The Last Piece

God bless you, Lynn!

Jessie Todd

The Last Piece

TERRIE TODD

The Last Piece

© 2021 by Terrie Todd

Published in association with the Books & Such Literary Management,
52 Mission Circle, Suite 122, PMB 170, Santa Rosa, CA 95409-5370,
www.booksandsuch.com.

Print ISBN: 9798503212167

Printed in the United States of America

Author photo: G. Loewen Photography

Dedicated with love to our grandsons

Keegan, Allistar, Rorin, Linus, Mattias

May you discover early that Jesus is, and always will be, the last piece to life's every puzzle.

Table of Contents

Part 1: 1937

Ray

Chapter One

R ay Matthews stared at the prairie landscape as the wheels made their hypnotic chug on the railway tracks below. For the next hour at least, he could allow the gentle rocking motion to lull him into a sort of oblivion. Into an alternate reality where the events of the last twenty-four hours were fairy tales and not truth. Where he was still in art school, scheduled to graduate in nine months. Where Dad was still the muscular, energetic man he'd always been—slinging hay bales from the dusty field onto the hay rack with the same ease required to swat a fly in his mother's farm kitchen.

Ray had never imagined for a moment that the formidable, faith-filled Nate Matthews could be here one day and gone the next. The larger-than-life man had been the center of everything, not just the Matthews family but the entire community of Wishing Well and all its three hundred and twenty-nine inhabitants. They must be reeling. Dad had been a rock, the glue that held the community together through the leanest, driest years they'd ever known. And though drought and depression still raged, Nate Matthews had defied all odds by finding a way for Ray to enroll in the University of Manitoba's art program and pursue his dreams.

Ray closed his eyes and tried to forget the brief telegram he'd read at least ten times before the words even began to sank in.

Had it really been just yesterday? If only the telephone lines had been strung to Wishing Well—or anywhere in rural Manitoba, for that matter. He'd be able to reach Mum and get the details. Clearly, she'd taken great pains to use as few words as possible. RETURN HOME ASAP. DAD DIED. HARVEST.

Whatever happened to Dad must have been both sudden and accidental. That Mum had found it necessary to include the word "harvest" could mean only one thing. Ray was expected to stay home, at least until the harvest was in.

Only three weeks had passed since he'd said goodbye to his parents and sister and returned to university for his final year. The guilt of leaving his family to finish the harvest without him had reared its head then. But Dad's parting words, like always, lifted the load. "Go make us proud, son."

Ray had barely had time to learn the names of his new professors when Mum's telegram arrived. He'd carried it with him into Professor Robertson's office and explained. The man was a good course counselor, but had no understanding of annual farming cycles or how bringing in the harvest was a life and death matter. He hailed from Toronto, where both a theater and a gallery bore his family name. In Professor Robertson's prestigious home, the arts were revered above all else.

Closing his eyes, Ray recalled the conversation as perfectly as if he still stood before the man's desk.

"I'm truly sorry for the loss of your father." Professor Robertson looked at Ray over the top of his wire-rimmed spectacles. "Take as long as you need to settle his affairs. I should think two weeks will be sufficient. Ask one of your classmates to stay in touch by telephone with your assignments. William Spencer would be a good choice."

"Sir...respectfully, there are no telephones in my area of the province."

The man stared at Ray for a moment while this sank in. "Well, mail, then. It will take longer, but you should be able to keep up. I'll allow you to hand everything in together upon your return."

Ray studied the tiled pattern on the floor. "Sir, I...I don't know when I'll be able to return. Harvest was in full swing when Dad passed, and I'll need to finish the job. My father grows potatoes." He didn't bother explaining that Dad had started out a wheat farmer but the drought was followed by grasshopper infestations and then, when he finally managed to grow a signif-icant crop, the price of wheat had dwindled to worthless. Nate Matthews had the wits, upon observing the success of his wife's garden potatoes, to plant them in his low-lying field. His well was also the deepest and most consistent water source for miles.

This time the professor removed his eyeglasses. Holding them in his right hand, he frowned. "You are a promising young artist, Matthews. Exceptional, I would say. You've won a spot at this institution coveted by many others. You've done so on the recommendation of trusted teachers who believed in you enough to help you land the scholarships that got you this far. You've won how many contests? Six? Seven?"

"Seven, sir."

"And at least two of those were international, if I remember right."

"Yes, sir." Ray focused on the painting on the wall behind Professor Robertson's desk, a landscape that had earned the man an award of his own.

"Now you're telling me you would toss all that away in order to pick vegetables? Don't be absurd, young man. We could give your seat to any number of willing takers in a heartbeat." He snapped his fingers.

Ray resisted the temptation to point out that potatoes are dug, not picked. "I know, sir. And I appreciate everything—I do. I want to return and complete my program. I just don't think I can be back that quickly."

"You do realize the deadline for any tuition refund just passed?"

Ray nodded. And since his dormitory and meals fees were paid monthly, there was nothing to collect there either.

The man gave Ray one final stare. "Two weeks. Or the spot goes to someone who can commit. Please extend my sympathy to your mother."

The train whistle dragged Ray back to the present.

"Wishing Well!" the porter called out.

Stretching for his belongings from the overhead compartment served to remind Ray that, while he'd inherited Dad's dark hair and eyes, his stature came from Mum's side. He pressed his face to the window. Would anyone be waiting for him on the platform? Most likely not. His return telegram to Mum had said only that he'd come as soon as he could.

The late-September sunshine warmed his face as he stepped down from the train. One look around confirmed that no one was there for him. He began the two-mile walk to the Matthews farm. The solitude would give him a chance to collect his thoughts in these familiar and comforting surroundings. Was it his imagination, or had the dust begun to settle since he left? After years of it, one got so used to daily grit in the eyes, teeth, and hair that it seemed normal. But today it was easy to breathe. Nothing obscured the sun except the odd fluffy cloud. Many of the fields he passed lay barren, but the ones that had been planted looked more promising than in previous years. Perhaps the worst was finally behind them.

The walk home would take him past the church and cemetery on the edge of town. Should he stop and see Sarah's grave? Common sense told him no. The sooner he got home, the sooner Mum would be relieved. And they would be burying Dad here in a day or two. He could always slip away to Sarah's grave afterward.

But as the rows of crosses and headstones came into view, Ray's feet seemed to take on a will of their own. He soon found himself standing at the grave of the woman he'd expected to share his life with. He knelt and brushed a small tumbleweed away from the stone, tossing it aside. He ran his hand over the simple engraving.

Sarah Grace Martindale
1913 – 1932

The stone displayed no date to mark her birthday, May 24. No date of death, though Ray would never forget that bitterly cold January 16. No scripture verse, though Sarah's favorite had been Psalm 46:10: "Be still and know that I am God." No hint as to the cause of death, though the pitiful sounds from her pneumonia-wracked lungs still rang in Ray's ears whenever he heard someone coughing. No epitaph to describe her, though she'd been the nearest thing to an angel this earth would ever see. Ray and Sarah had been sweethearts from the time they were old enough to understand what the word meant, and they'd planned a spring wedding for exactly three months after the day she died.

"Hello, Sarah." Ray's words were barely audible. "I came home sooner than expected. But you probably know that. You probably know Dad's up there now too. Have you seen him yet? If so, I envy him a little."

He looked around the peaceful setting. The little church he'd attended all his life still held its steeple high, though sandstorms had peeled most of the white paint away. Despite the lack of green grass and flowers, the cemetery had remained pretty in its own way. Sparrows twittered from the evergreens that provided shelter along three sides. A mourning dove cooed. *How fitting.*

"I don't know how I'm going to do it, Sarah. Mum's going to need me to take over full-time, and you know I was never that great a farmer. Not like Dad. He had the strength and stamina of three men. Oh, I can do the work, and I will. I'll give it my best shot, anyway. But my heart will never be in it. Dad knew that, and I know you did too. If it hadn't been for you and for him, I'd never have gone to art school. Now you're both gone. And I'm pretty sure it's the end of school for me too." His gaze returned to the stone.

"I sure wish you were here. We'd have celebrated our second anniversary already, you realize that? Would we have a little one by now? I could handle this if you were here. I could handle anything. Anyway…" He stood and tapped his hat against his pant leg before returning it to his head. "I need to get home. I love you, girl."

Back on the road, Ray stepped up his pace and turned his thoughts toward the farm and all the work that surely awaited him there. With half a mile to go, a horn startled him, making him turn around. From the shape of the driver's beat-up old straw hat, Ray recognized their neighbor and one of his father's good friends, Eli Robinson. Eli stopped his old Ford truck and leaned across the passenger seat. "That you, Ray? Hop in." He cleared some sundry junk from the seat, then swiped a sleeve across his whiskered cheek.

Without a word, Ray tossed his bags into the back of Eli's truck and climbed into the cab where the scents of burlap, sweat, and something he couldn't identify combined to make him glad the windows were rolled down. Eli put the truck back in gear and continued down the road toward home, which would take him right past the Matthews farm.

"Figured you'd be coming home today." Eli kept his eyes on the gravel road. "Real sorry about your dad."

"Thank you."

Nothing more was said, nor needed to be. Eli turned down the Matthews' lane and pulled up in front of the old house. Chickens scattered. Uncle Henry's Chevy was parked next to Dad's pickup truck in the yard. Old Barney, the mutt that Mum and Dad had presented to him as a pup on his twelfth birthday, lumbered over with a wagging tail.

"Sure appreciate the ride." Ray climbed out and began rubbing Barney behind the ears. "Hey there, boy."

"Think nothing of it. I was going right by." Eli's tone held compassion. "Please tell your mother how sorry I am. He was a good man."

"I will. Thanks." Ray watched his neighbor drive away. When he turned around, Mum and Caroline stood on the side porch. He hadn't even heard the door open. For a moment, he felt frozen to the spot. Who was this woman, this girl? Mum looked more like his grandmother. Stooped. Wrinkled. And oh, so very weary.

And was it possible Caroline could have gotten even thinner? His sister had always been small for her age, but at fifteen, she should be showing the graceful curves of a young woman. Instead, she reminded Ray of the scarecrow they put up every year in Mum's garden. Not that he'd say such a horrible thing aloud, not to anyone.

Both women showed signs of recent weeping—swollen, red eyes above dark circles. Guilt and grief wrestled for the top spot in Ray's chest, paralyzing him. If only he could snap his fingers and be back in Winnipeg, in one of his art classes, focused on a project. If only none of this was true. If only his family was happy and thriving.

"Raymond."

The sound of his name from Mum's lips finally moved Ray to action, and he walked the few steps to the porch. He set his bags down to embrace Mum first, then Caroline.

"What happened?" His voice was little more than a weak croak. Still, no tears came.

"Come inside." Mum held the door open while Ray passed through with his bags. "Say hello to everyone, and then we'll talk."

The familiar smell of home wrapped Ray in a comforting hug as he stepped into the kitchen. More food burdened the table than he'd eaten in weeks—sliced roast beef and ham, deviled eggs, homemade breads, cakes, and bowls of garden vegetables. A pot of soup simmered on Mum's woodstove, releasing the soothing fragrance of potatoes and celery. His neighbors and relatives had sacrificed greatly to share their food when they all had so little. The obvious acts of kindness touched his heart.

Subdued voices came from the living room, and someone spoke his name.

Mum led him toward the entrance. "Ray's here."

Ray stood in the arched doorway and scanned the room. Aunts, uncles, cousins, and neighbors occupied every seat. Dad's younger brother looked so much like Dad, it almost took Ray's breath away.

He managed a weak smile. "Hi, everybody. Thanks for being here."

The next few minutes were a blur of awkward hugs and words.

"So sorry, Raymond. So very sorry."

"You must be famished. What would you like?"

"I can fill you a plate."

"Thank you." Ray looked at Mum, who nodded in the direction of the stairs. He grabbed his bags and followed her up to his room. They sat side by side on the edge of his bed.

"What happened to Dad?" Ray had imagined all sorts of awful things, from Dad being trampled and dragged by his team of horses to somehow becoming trapped under a tractor tire.

"It was his heart. Doc says he probably had a congenital heart problem all along. It just never showed up before."

Had he misheard? Dad had a bad heart? "But...he was so strong."

"I know." Mum shook her head. "I'm still in shock too. He'd put in a long day, like always. When he finally came in around ten, I gave him his supper. He only ate a couple of bites. He was unusually quiet. Said he was going straight to bed. I stayed up to finish a few things—I'd been canning tomatoes and wanted to get the jars on the cellar shelves. When I came to bed around eleven, I couldn't hear him breathing. Normally, he'd be snoring by that time. I listened awhile then called him softly. Then more loudly. No response." Her voice cracked, but she cleared her throat and kept sharing her story. "Finally, I lit a lamp. I shook him. But he was gone. He was gone and I hadn't heard a thing. I don't know if he struggled. I didn't have a chance to say goodbye!" She began to sob.

Ray wrapped his arms around her as she leaned into his chest. If only he could cry like that. What could he say to comfort her? Memories of losing Sarah rose to the surface. If his own heart stopped that day, how much worse must it be after twenty-five years of marriage? He held Mum close, gently rubbing her back and shoulder until the sobbing subsided.

"I'm so glad you're here, Ray. I don't know what I'm going to do. I'm just so...bewildered."

"It'll be all right. We don't have to figure it all out today. Let's just focus on laying Dad to rest. Then, the next thing will be finishing the harvest. I'm here now. Try not to worry."

Even as he spoke the reassuring words, Ray's confidence sagged. "Laying Dad to rest" sounded disrespectful. Dad had never been inactive a day in his life. He'd worked hard and played harder, when he got the rare opportunity to do so. More importantly, his faith in God was steadfast as a rock. Ray had no doubt that Dad was with the Lord and that whatever he was doing right now, it wasn't resting.

Mum let out a big sigh. "I should go back down. Don't take too long. Your aunties will have your plate heaping with food by now." She stood and crossed the room.

"Be down in a minute."

After Mum left, her shoulders a little straighter and chin a little higher than when he'd first arrived, Ray drew a deep breath. How strange to be sitting here again.

The toy tractor Dad had carved when Ray was five sat atop his dresser, its moving parts still in perfect order. An assortment of art-related books crowded a bookcase on the other wall. *How to Sketch ... Drawing Faces ... The Works of Van Gogh*. All had been Christmas and birthday presents over the years. The quilt on which he sat had been lovingly pieced together by Grandma and handed down to Mum when she married. The curtains at the window were Mum's handiwork—plaid fabric in navy, red, and yellow. Everything in here offered comfort and belonging. But the painting over his bed made his pulse speed up. He'd finished the portrait of Sarah for her eighteenth birthday and surprised her with it.

Her face had lit up. He could still hear her. "Ray! I don't know what to say."

He'd portrayed her in a garden, gazing down into a flower-laden wishing well, with more flowers in her hair. The well was only figurative. Though their little town had been named Wishing Well, no one seemed to know why or where there might have been such a well. Sarah's dream from the age of twelve had been to raise funds to build a lovely wishing well in the town square. She'd lobbied the town council and solicited donations. She'd organized fundraisers. But the Depression had made Sarah's well a low priority. When she passed away, the fund was donated to her family so they could afford a decent burial and headstone. Sarah's parents had given the painting back to Ray.

"You should keep it," he'd told them.

"No," Mrs. Martindale had insisted. "It's lovely. You captured her essence perfectly. But there is still no wishing well in this town, and every time I see the portrait, it's a reminder that we failed her. I can't bear the pain of it."

Just like he couldn't bear this pain now. He gazed into the likeness of his Sarah's eyes, the windows to her gentle soul, and whispered softly. "Tell Jesus I need his help desperately, Sarah. Please."

With a sigh, he stood and returned downstairs, leaving his suitcases behind—still packed.

Chapter Two

Christmas had come.

For Caroline's sake, Ray and Mum agreed they should have a tree and make things as normal as possible. Now Ray squinted at the little candles Mum and Caroline had clipped onto the branches. Each evening, they lit them for ten minutes and sat quietly or softly sang *Silent Night* or *O Little Town of Bethlehem*. Sometimes, they talked about Dad. Caroline was convinced their father now sat under the most glorious Christmas tree imaginable. She described it with enthusiasm and conviction. Ray was happy to listen.

"It's at least a hundred feet tall and greener than any green you have seen here on earth. The decorations are real live angels who give off such a glow you nearly have to shade your eyes to look." Her blue eyes shimmered as she spoke. "They are wearing every color in the rainbow, and even some colors we've never heard of, and when they fly around, it's like the whole tree is in motion. It's alive, of course, not cut. And when the angels sing, it's a birthday song to Jesus—more magnificent than anything our ears can imagine. Daddy's up there, taking it all in and laughing at the wonder of it." She looked at him. "Sarah is there, too. She's singing along."

Even if Caroline's imagination ran nowhere close to reality, Ray saw no reason to challenge her. On the contrary, it was comforting to picture such a thing. And despite their loss, the little family had much to be grateful for. With the help of neighbors and extended family, they'd harvested Dad's potatoes and sold them for enough to pay some bills—including the undertaker's. As he'd expected, Ray had not returned to school. He'd already resigned himself to his education being over when the official letter arrived from the university. His spot had been given to another student.

They never talked about it. After her initial tears, Mum had remained stoic. The only contrary words from her came whenever Ray referred to the land, the tractor, the potato picker, or the horses as "Dad's."

"They're yours now, son. It's all yours. You mustn't forget."

All mine. Ray stared at the burning candles and let the idea sink in. He didn't want to be ungrateful, but the inheritance felt like a heavy burden. If it were "all his," that meant the remaining debts, the responsibility, and the risks were all his too. All he really wanted was to return to his painting, but he hadn't touched a brush since Dad's death. There simply wasn't time. He had watched Dad work with the strength of an ox from the pre-dawn hours until after dark. Only on Sundays did he rest, and Ray remembered many a Sunday afternoon spent cutting seed potatoes with the family on the front porch.

"Go ahead and open it." Mum's voice interrupted Ray's thoughts. Caroline had picked up the one gift that sat beneath their tree, the one they had agreed they couldn't do without. Though they all knew what it was, only Mum knew the details. She'd already cleared the corner table for their annual tradition— a jigsaw puzzle to be started Christmas Eve and completed on Christmas Day.

The jagged-cut puzzles had become the biggest rage after the Great Depression began—an affordable form of family entertainment that could be passed around the community until every family had assembled and unassembled it. Some of the wooden puzzles were finished and taken apart more than once per household. Dad had loved them from the moment he laid eyes on them on the shelf of Sellinger's General Store and was probably the first in Wishing Well to lay down the nickel required to rent a puzzle for a week. That was the same year he began buying a puzzle for Christmas each year for the family to assemble together and then pass around. The delight on his neighbors' faces when Nate Matthews would bring them a puzzle stuck with Ray. It didn't match the glow on Dad's face, though, knowing he was providing an extravagance the neighbors could never afford.

Caroline untied the red string from the package, rolled it carefully into a ball, and handed it to Mum, who would return it to her string jar. Then she unfolded the brown paper to expose the puzzle box. The picture on the front revealed what the assembled jigsaw would look like—a white farmhouse with green shutters on every window and red geraniums in every window box. The front porch invited the viewer to come sit on one of its two red rockers. Vivid green grass surrounded the house, and a swing hung from a large tree in the yard. A black-and-white dog made his way from the house to a big red barn, where yellow hay spilled out from an upper loft. Golden fields ripe for harvest filled the background, under a blue sky with a smattering of fluffy white clouds.

"Your father would have loved it." Mum ran her hand over the box's surface. "I picked it out because this was his dream— that life could be like this one day."

The picture was such a contrast to the reality of the last several years, with the dust storms that had left the ground parched and the buildings stripped of color. The artist who painted it was probably in cahoots with the company who sold it, knowing how it would appeal to farm folks who clung staunchly to their dreams despite the odds.

Mum moved the oil lamp to the table while Caroline opened the box and emptied the contents onto the surface. They turned all the pieces right-side up and began organizing them. By the time they'd completed all four edges, it was eleven o'clock.

"We'd best turn in." Mum yawned.

No one had said what Ray knew they were all thinking. Assembling the jigsaw puzzle was not the same without Dad's constant comments and laughter.

Christmas morning dawned bright and frigid. Ray was the first to rise, and he hustled to get a fire roaring in Mum's cook stove. By the time she came downstairs, the kitchen was toasty. He bundled up in Dad's warmest chore clothes and stepped out into air so cold it sucked his breath away. He ran to the chicken coop and hastened inside to not let in any more cold than necessary. The birds huddled together. Ray had taken Mum's advice and fed them corn the night before to help them stay warm through the night. He filled their feeder, then knocked the ice from their water pan and refilled it from the pail he'd brought from the house— warm water scooped from the reservoir on the back of the stove. He didn't expect any eggs in this weather but found three. Gently, he tucked them into his pockets before heading to the barn.

Daisy waited patiently to be milked, and the warmth of her body kept Ray comfortable as he leaned his head into her side. With the milking done, he pitched fresh hay down from the loft for Daisy and for Dad's two horses in the opposite stalls. He wouldn't be turning any of the animals out today.

Porridge bubbled on the stove when he returned to the house.

"Merry Christmas, Mum." Ray pulled the eggs from his pockets and held them out.

She smiled. "It's a miracle! How do we want them?"

"Poached!" Ray and Caroline answered in unison. His sister was setting the table, wrapped in a chenille robe over a heavy flannel nightgown, with thick woolen socks on her feet.

The sunshine streaming through the kitchen window made her mussed hair look like a halo around her face. Ray tugged at one of her day-old braids as he passed her.

When all was ready, the three of them sat at the table Caroline had made extra festive by pulling down Mother's best dishes and lacy tablecloth. The table was round, and ever since Dad's passing, Caroline had been setting their plates an equal distance apart around it and moving Dad's chair to the corner of the kitchen. Clearly, she hoped it would make Dad's absence less obvious, as if it ever could. After the meal, Mum always rearranged the chairs, replacing the fourth one in its usual spot. As far as Ray knew, they never discussed the little ritual.

"Lord…" Mum began the grace, her hands folded. "Thank you for another Christmas and for the gift of your son, our redeemer, Jesus. Bless all at this table and in our community today. May no one go hungry or cold. Amen."

They really did have much to be grateful for. Though the pain of losing Dad remained raw and the disappointment of quitting school hung on him like a weighted cloak, their family still had things so much better than many.

With full tummies, they spent the day working on the puzzle that depicted Dad's ideal life. By four in the afternoon, shadows lengthened, and the time for evening chores drew near. The puzzle was only three-quarters complete.

"It can wait for another day." Mum sighed. "My eyes are worn out. Besides, we still have a long winter ahead."

"And your daughter has, no doubt, already pocketed the last piece." Ray grinned at Caroline. It was a tradition for her to remove one piece and hang onto it, just for the joy of plopping in the last one to complete the picture. Ray found it annoying but loved her too much to truly mind.

Caroline grinned sheepishly. "Wouldn't you like to know?"

"You're lucky we're not easily angered. Someday, you're going to pull that stunt with someone who doesn't think you're so darling. *Then* you'll be in trouble."

"Ray." Mum gave him a grin. "Let her have her fun."

When Ray returned to the house with the evening's milk, a simple supper waited on the table. Potato soup and bread. It was a far cry from the turkey dinner with all the trimmings they'd enjoyed in more prosperous years, but those were a dim memory, anyway. As long as they had their own milk, eggs, and potatoes, they would never go hungry.

"I'll be taking the train to the city early in the new year," Ray announced after he had said grace. "I have some loose ends to tie up. Should be able to get it all done and come home the same day." He'd left a few belongings with his roommate at the university, with a glimmer of hope that he'd be returning. The roommate had written to say the items were waiting in a box in the dean's office, since he'd had to make space for a new student.

"When?" Mother buttered her bread.

"Registration day for the new session, if I can. I'd like to sell my textbooks while I have the chance. There's bound to be a student who needs them and will appreciate a discounted price. And I can bring home the rest of my clothes and paintbrushes."

His mother swallowed and nodded her head. Not once had she hinted that Ray would ever return to school, and he had no reason to think she understood how deep a loss he felt.

"Can I come? Please-oh-please?" Caroline's eyes were bright at the prospect. "School doesn't start until January seventh."

"Whatever for?" The tone of Mother's voice said it all—the price of a ticket for Caroline to tag along would be a complete waste.

"For the adventure! I want to see everything—the electric trolleys and the legislative building and what's in the shop windows."

Ray grinned. "It's not like you think, Sis. From the train station, I catch a bus to Fort Garry. The university sits on a big farm, basically. It's not that different from home."

"Well, at least I'll see Union Station. It's magnificent!"

"How would you know?" Ray teased.

"Teacher showed us pictures. It's got a glorious dome in the center and fancy pillars and marble floor, with circular designs in it." Caroline motioned with her hands as though she were painting the designs herself. "And if we go soon enough, there might even be a big Christmas tree in the center!"

Mum snorted. "It's not that grand. Besides, what if you had one of your attacks?"

Carolyn wouldn't give up that easily. "Ray knows what to do. Don't you, Ray?"

Ray could imagine running his errands with Caroline in tow, gawking at everything in sight. He had to agree with Mum even while sympathizing with his sister. "Maybe another time. When the weather's nice. We can pack a picnic and take our time."

Caroline sighed. "You say that now. It'll never happen."

Mum rolled her eyes. "Oh, don't be such a princess. Finish your soup."

Ray gave Caroline a compassionate grin. Inwardly, he sighed with relief. He hadn't mentioned his biggest reason for wanting to return to the university or the paintings he'd left behind. If Professor Robertson could help him find a buyer, he might bring home a lot more money than whatever his textbooks generated. Though the farm bills were nearly paid, nothing remained to get the family through until next harvest, let alone to buy seed. If they couldn't plant, there would be no next harvest.

Chapter Three

These are excellent, Matthews." Professor Robertson's head nodded as he studied the five paintings Ray had laid out. "Really top notch. And I wish so much I could give you hope, but with the Depression—"

"I know." Ray was so sick of that word. Would it never end? "No one is buying right now. I understand." He began to pack up his paintings.

"Well, not exactly *no one.*"

Ray paused and looked up.

"Back in November, our school had a visit from a manufacturer of jigsaw puzzles." He sat at his desk and picked up a pipe that rested there. "Silly fad. But they're willing to buy pictures done by students. I encouraged it as a way for art students to get exposure for their work."

Ray listened with interest, waiting while the man lit his pipe and relaxed back into his chair. "The pay is abysmal, I'm afraid. But if a particular artist's work proves popular, they may be able to sell their next piece for more."

"That would be great! I'm not a student anymore, though. Does that matter?"

"I don't think so." The professor pulled a business card from his desk drawer. "In my opinion, a jigsaw puzzle would be a sorry use for your work, Matthews. I wouldn't even tell you about this if you weren't so desperate to sell. I do hope this nasty economy turns 'round soon. I see a much brighter future for you than this."

"Thank you, sir." Ray took the card and studied it. **Merry Times Amusements**. *See your art turned into a beautiful jigsaw puzzle! Offering premium prices for your paintings.* The address was a number on Donald Street. Only a few blocks from Union Station. If Ray hurried, he could arrive in plenty of time to see someone before catching his train back to Wishing Well.

But first, he had a stop to make. At the university bookstore, a clerk bought back his textbooks for half of what Ray had paid. He could have made more by selling directly to a student and still given that student a better deal, but time was of the essence. He pocketed the money. Glad to have only his case of paintings to carry, he hurried to the bus stop to catch the next ride back to the city. It was a mild day for January, but students still hunched in their woolen toques and mittens, shifting their weight from one foot to the other to keep warm until the bus came.

How "abysmal" a price might the puzzle company pay? Ray had seen paintings priced as high as fifty dollars when their class visited the art gallery. Dare he hope for twenty? Any amount would help with the expenses at home, and he certainly didn't want to haul these paintings all the way back there. Cash in the pocket, no matter how little, would always be better. Still, if he could get even ten dollars for each of his five pictures, he'd have fifty plus the money from his textbooks. Enough to pay the rest of the bills *and* buy seed come planting time.

The bus took him right to Donald Street, and Ray found the number he was looking for. On the second floor, he found a door with a glass window on which was painted *Merry Times Amusements* followed by the hours they kept. Inside, several assembled jigsaw puzzles graced the walls. Everything from simple cartoon drawings to more complicated landscapes to depictions of brand-name products had been framed and hung. The pictures boosted his confidence, as most of them were inferior work to his own. He was sure of it. In the middle of the room, two desks sat side by side. At the one on the right, a balding man with rolled-up sleeves spoke rapidly on the telephone while a cigarette smoldered from an overflowing ashtray on his desktop. At the other, a young woman with reddish hair looked up from her typewriter and raised lovely blue eyes in Ray's direction.

"May I help you?"

"Good afternoon. My name is Ray Matthews. I've recently been an art student at the University of Manitoba. I'm here at the suggestion of Professor Robertson."

She glanced at Ray's case. "You have some work to sell, have you?"

"Yes."

"Mr. Rawlings will need to take a look." She nodded in the direction of the man beside her. "But while you're waiting, you can come around here and lay it all out for him." She stood, inviting Ray to follow her to two long tables against the back wall of the room. One was empty. The other held one painting of a little boy with a dog. "Feel free to arrange your pieces how you like, and if you're done before he's ready, just take a seat."

"Thank you." Ray wiped the palms of his hands on the front of his trousers and undid the latch on his art case. He pulled out the five pieces of canvas, one at a time, and laid them carefully on the table. Then he rearranged them, stood back, and rearranged again. All five pieces had been assignments for classes and were completely different from each other. An ink rendering of the Manitoba Union building on campus. An oil painting of a wheat field ripe for harvest. A watercolor still life of his mother's canning jars all in a row—tomatoes, pickles, green beans, plums, saskatoons. A pastel sketch of a shelf of books in the university library. And his personal favorite, Caroline seated on a swing, her hair in messy braids and her bare feet dragging in the dirt below. He wouldn't part with it except that Caroline wouldn't appreciate the piece at all. "Makes me look like a baby," she'd say with a toss of her head. He could almost hear her.

Ray was just about to rearrange the pieces a third time when he heard the man hang up the telephone and rise from his chair.

"Well, well. What have we here?" He held out one hand in Ray's direction while his eyes perused the artwork.

"Ray Matthews, sir." Ray shook the man's hand. "I'm here on Professor Robertson's recommendation."

"John Rawlings." He looked Ray up and down, then turned back to the table. "Not bad work, son. Not the best I've seen, of course." He took a long drag from his cigarette.

"No, I wouldn't expect so." Ray shifted awkwardly.

"The preserves would work well for a puzzle. Lots of color. This one, too." He pointed at the picture of Caroline. "Folks love this stuff." He stood back and rocked on his heels. "Tell you what. I'll give you five dollars each for those two, and two dollars for each of the others."

Ray's heart sank. Sixteen dollars. He chewed on his bottom lip for a moment. Did he dare dicker with the man when he'd never sold one painting before in his whole life? A faint cough from the receptionist's desk prompted him to glance her way. She seemed to be looking at Ray out of the corner of her eye even though she faced her typewriter. Was that a slight shake of her head, or was he imagining it?

"C'mon, young man, I don't have all day." Mr. Rawlings leaned toward his desk to stub out his cigarette.

Deeply hoping he wouldn't regret the bold move, Ray began packing all but the two paintings for which he'd been offered five dollars. "I'll just keep these three, then." His heart pounded. He was throwing away the opportunity to collect six dollars, and he'd have to carry the paintings all the way home on the train. What possible good would they do stacked in a closet or even hanging on his mother's walls? Should he back down?

"Wait a minute." Mr. Rawlings turned back. "Let me see those again. I didn't get a really good look."

Ray glanced back at the woman as a small smirk turned her lips up, although she remained focused on her work. He returned the rejected paintings to the table with his others.

Mr. Rawlings studied them more carefully this time. "That wheat field would be quite a challenge. Some people like the harder ones. I suppose those books would work out all right too."

Ray waited.

"Got plans for after graduation?"

Ray wasn't sure how to respond. If the man knew he was no longer a student and would not be completing school, would it matter? "N-no. Not yet. Not really," he stammered. It wasn't a lie, exactly.

"Got more of these somewhere?"

Ray thought of the stack of canvasses leaning against the wall in his bedroom closet back home. "Yes, sir. Back home in Wishing Well."

"Are they as good as these?"

Ray didn't think they were, and was about to say so, but Mr. Rawlings pivoted on his heel and headed toward the hat rack in the corner by the door. While he put on his coat, he said, "Miss Cook, give the man twenty-five dollars for the lot of them, and be sure to get his address. I've got a meeting I must get to." He added his hat and, with his hand on the doorknob, turned back one last time to glance at Ray. "That's my final offer. Good day, young man. Come back when you can bring me more."

The door closed behind him, and Ray looked at Miss Cook, who smiled broadly now.

"Congratulations, Mr. Matthews. Feel free to sit down while I prepare your receipt. I'll only be a minute." She disappeared through a door off to the side.

Instead of sitting, Ray circled the room, examining each framed jigsaw puzzle more closely. When Miss Cook returned, she carried cash in her hand and counted out five five-dollar bills as she laid them on her desk. Then she pulled a receipt book from her desk drawer and filled it out for Ray to sign.

"Your paintings are very good." She turned the book around and handed Ray a fountain pen.

"Thank you." He signed on the line and picked up the cash. "An art fan, are you?"

"Oh, not especially. I'm just a secretary—and thankful to have a job in these tough times. When it comes to pictures, I just know what I like."

"Do you have a favorite?" Ray waved his hand to indicate the puzzles on the walls.

Miss Cook glanced around. "Yes." She stood and turned to where Ray's paintings still lay on display, then tapped her lips with one finger while she looked at them. "This one."

She was pointing at the picture of Caroline. Ray chuckled. "I'll tell my little sister you said so, although she'd hate that picture."

"Is it her?"

"It's how I see her."

"What's her name?" She picked up the painting in both hands and held it at arm's length.

"Caroline. She hates that, too, come to think of it."

"A contrary one, is she?" Miss Cook laid the painting down and returned to her chair.

"Just spunky. She's all heart when you get to know her." Ray returned his wallet to his pocket. "Well, thank you ... for *every*thing." Tempted to suggest she'd encouraged him to hold out for more money, he didn't want to place her in an awkward position. "I appreciate it."

"Good luck to you."

"Thank you. I have a train to catch."

"Maybe we'll see you back?"

"Yes, maybe."

Ray left the office and ran all the way to Union Station to make the four-fifteen train for Wishing Well before he changed his mind.

Chapter Four

Ray arrived at the farm to Daisy's bellowing, a clear indication she was in dire need of milking. As he entered the house, the familiar scent of camphor struck him, and humidity hung heavy in the air. On his mother's woodstove, the kettle released a slow, steady whistle of steam.

Oh no.

It could only mean Caroline's breathing was in trouble again. She'd made it through the dusty harvest season with no attacks, and they had all begun to hope she'd finally outgrown her problems. His sister's coughing drew him to the living room and he crossed the kitchen without removing his boots.

"Is it bad?"

His mother leaned over Caroline as she lay on the sofa, her breathing labored. She looked up. "Oh, Ray. Thank God. I know the chores need doing, but I didn't want to leave her."

"I'll get to it right away. How long's she been like this?" Caroline had still been asleep when he'd left for Winnipeg that morning.

"Most of the day."

Caroline stopped coughing long enough to say, "Hi, Ray. What's new in the city?" She coughed some more.

Mum ran her hand through Caroline's hair. "Don't try to talk, love. It only makes it worse."

Ray gave his sister a big smile. "When I get in from chores, I'll tell you all about it—if you promise not to talk." He pulled out his wallet and removed all the money he'd collected that day. "Look, Mum. I did all right."

Mum looked at the money but didn't reach for it. "Oh, Ray. That's wonderful. Tomorrow you can take it to town and take care of a few bills. Caroline's medicine is running low too."

When Ray returned to the house after chores, Caroline had fallen asleep, her breathing regular and quiet. The worst was over. Mum looked up from the chair she'd been dozing in.

"Want me to sit up with her so you can get some sleep?" Ray whispered.

Mum shook her head. "You've had a long day. Go get some rest."

"Don't stay up too late." Ray climbed the stairs, weariness making his legs heavy. Resisting the temptation to fall straight into bed, he knelt on the floor a moment, elbows resting on the edge of the mattress.

"Lord, thanks for the money I was able to bring home today. Thank you for seeing Caroline through another one of her spells. Please strengthen her. And Mum." He pulled the quilt back and prepared to climb into bed, but at the last second resumed his pose to pray two more words: "And me."

As soon as morning chores were done, Ray started up Dad's truck and headed to town, money in his wallet. First, he visited the pharmacy to fill Caroline's prescription. With her medicine safely in his pocket, he made two stops to pay off some overdue bills. The potato picker had required a new part halfway through harvest, and the farm fuel tank had been filled on credit. With those debts cleared, Ray walked down the street with a lighter heart than he'd felt in weeks—maybe months. He even had six dollars left over to deposit in the bank, right after he stopped at the post office.

"Morning!" Ray greeted the postmaster. "Any mail for us?"

The elderly gentleman shuffled off to a wall covered with cubbyholes and searched until he found the one marked *Matthews, Nathanael.* Dad's name had still not been removed from the family mailbox.

"Just one. Registered." The postmaster gave Ray a journal and showed him which line to sign on, then handed the letter through the wicket to Ray. "How's your mother and sister?"

"They're all right. Thanks for asking." The letter was from the bank, addressed to his mother. *They could have saved themselves a stamp since I'm on my way there.* He stepped away from the wicket and opened the envelope to reveal a one-page, type-written letter with the Bank of Canada's official logo at the top.

> *Dear Mrs. Matthews,*
>
> *This is our third letter informing you that the mortgage taken out by your late husband on March 16, 1937, became due upon his passing last September. While the untimely death of Mr. Matthews is most unfortunate, the bank can no longer continue to carry this debt. Since we have received no reply from you, we regret we have been forced to begin foreclosure proceedings …*

Ray didn't bother reading to the end. He shoved the letter into his pocket as he headed out the door and down the street to the bank. This had to be a mistake. Dad had inherited the land from *his* father, debt-free—the main reason they'd always done better than others in the community. Perhaps the bank was sending out so many foreclosure letters these days, they'd gotten mixed up and sent Mum one as well. Nothing else made sense.

A male customer stood at the lone wicket when he entered the Wishing Well branch of the Bank of Canada. Ray nodded to him as he finished his business and moved aside to give Ray room.

The teller, an old classmate of Ray's named Susan, greeted him with a warm smile. "Hello, Ray. What can I help you with today?"

"I'm afraid there's been a bit of a mix-up, Susan." He pulled the letter from his pocket and checked the signature at the bottom. "I wonder if I might be able to see Mr. Wiggins to clear it up."

Susan glanced at the letter, then back at Ray. "I'll see if he's available."

"Thanks." While he waited, Ray read the letter to the end. Why would Dad have taken out a mortgage on the farm? And why did they say this was their third letter when this was the first he'd heard of it? It made no sense. Hopefully, he could straighten things out without involving Mum. She didn't need this on top of everything else.

"Mr. Wiggins will see you now." Susan opened a little gate in the countertop to let Ray through. He removed his hat as he entered the bank manager's office.

Mr. Wiggins rose from his desk. "Good morning, Mr. Matthews. I'm glad you've come in. Have a seat. Can I call you Raymond?"

Ray nodded and sat at one of two chairs facing the man's desk. He placed his hat on his knee. Before he could speak, the bank manager continued.

"You're here about the foreclosure."

"That's right. I only now received this letter. Obviously, there's been a mistake, and I'd like to clear things up." Ray paused to clear his throat. "I know you're fairly new here, so you might not be as familiar with our family's history as the previous manager. My father's farm was always free and clear. That's one of the things that kept it viable through the last decade when so many others were losing theirs—"

Mr. Wiggins held up a hand to stop him. "Before you continue, Raymond—you are only partly correct. I'm sorry if your father didn't keep you abreast of his business dealings, but the truth is, his farm was in as much jeopardy as many others. The difference was, we agreed to mortgage his farm at a time when we were refusing others precisely because of his previous debt-free status *and* his reputation for being an exceptionally hard-working, strong man."

"That he was."

"He was also a generous man."

"Yes, he was. But I don't see how that—"

"A little too generous sometimes. Are you aware he helped out several of his neighbors in the early part of this decade?"

"Well, sure." Ray recalled with pride some of the stories that had come out at Dad's funeral. It seemed the whole community saw him as someone who would go above and beyond the call of duty to lend a hand, or a dollar. "Dad was always helping where he could, but—"

"To a fault, Raymond. When he mortgaged the farm, he didn't use the money only to finance his own operation, but he shared it with his neighbors. Sometimes, he paid their bills anonymously, and I'd hear about it from merchants who were also in desperate danger of losing *their* businesses."

Ray was not completely shocked. Dad had derived great joy from helping others and would have given the shirt off his back.

"It made him quite the hero, but it wasn't shrewd business." Mr. Wiggins moved some papers on his desk. "It was probably this tendency that made him come see us in the first place. He might have been all right otherwise. In any case, the man was his own collateral. We were betting on his abilities and reputation—as was he. Sadly, we all lost the bet."

How could the man be so cold? "But—this makes no sense. Why did my mother not know anything about this? The letter says this is the third notice." He waved it in the air.

Mr. Wiggins nodded. "Frankly, we've become used to customers not responding to those letters. Usually, by the time we arrive at their farm, the place is deserted. They've left without a trace."

Ray stared at the man. Finally, he found his voice. "I came home from university as soon as my father passed, Mr. Wiggins. We finished the harvest without him, and our bills are current. We even have a little set aside for next year's seed. If you come out to our farm, you'll see we're still very much in business."

"Well, then, there should be no problem paying off the mortgage."

Ray shook his head, searching the floor as if the answer could be found there.

"Did your father have a life insurance policy?"

"Life insurance?" If he had, Mum surely would have mentioned it by now. "I very much doubt it."

"It sounds as though you need to have a conversation with your mother, Raymond." He flipped a page in the daybook on his desk. "Can the two of you come back to see me together, say...Friday at ten?"

Ray blinked rapidly. Surely, this man could see the bank had nothing to gain by swooping in and laying claim to the farm. Who else would want it, or if they did, could afford to buy it? The room spun as he stood. "All r-right," he stammered. "Friday, then."

Ray drove slowly home. How was he going to tell Mum? How could he not have known what was happening? He should have taken better care of things. He clearly had a lot of growing up to do before he was ready to be the man of the family.

It wasn't until he pulled into the yard that he remembered the six dollars still in his wallet. At least the bank couldn't get their hands on it.

Chapter Five

When he arrived home and stepped into the kitchen, Ray found the house quiet and the main floor deserted. Mum had never been known to sleep during the day unless one of Caroline's attacks had kept her up all night. He closed the door softly behind him and tiptoed to the bottom of the stairs to listen for any stirring from above. Convinced they both must be asleep, he hung up his coat and rubbed his hands together over the stove.

Carefully, he pulled down the old Bee Hive golden corn syrup tin from a shelf above the table. Dad had used the tin to hold receipts and bills for as long as Ray could remember. Perhaps there'd be some clue inside. He pried off the lid and found the tin so jam-packed, he had to gently wiggle and tug each item out one by one.

He didn't need to look long. Two envelopes from the Bank of Canada had been tightly rolled up like cigarettes. They tried to stay that shape as Ray unrolled them with a sinking heart. Both were registered letters. Both had been signed for. Neither had been opened.

The postmarks told the story. The first letter had been mailed about two weeks after Dad's death, the second in early November. Mum must have suspected they held bad news and had chosen to remain in the dark, like the proverbial ostrich with its head in the sand. Ray wanted to pound his fist on the table. He wasn't sure who he felt angrier with right now, Mum or Dad.

A creak on the stairs made him jump, and he turned as Mum descended the last three steps. Her gaze went from the tin to Ray's face and back to the tin again. Without a word, she moved to the stove and stuffed in more wood. Ray stood frozen, watching her, the letters in his hand.

"I've been meaning to open those." Mum pulled down her teapot. "Just haven't got around to it yet."

"Another came today." Ray pulled it out of his pocket. "We're in trouble, Mum. Why didn't you tell me Dad mortgaged the farm?"

She whirled around to face him. "What?"

He swallowed hard. "You didn't know?"

By the sudden paleness of her face, she hadn't.

"Come here." He pulled a chair away from the table, and they both sat. Ray pushed the two older letters toward her, then tapped his finger on the new one. "This one came today. I went to see Mr. Wiggins at the bank. They want to foreclose on the farm."

With a trembling hand, Mum took the letter and read it. "I was afraid it might be something like this. Your father didn't tell me, but ... I trusted him. I figured everything would work out, that whatever was in those letters ... oh, I don't know. I've never been one for business."

They each opened one of the earlier letters and found them just as Mr. Wiggins had said. Due warning, sent by registered mail.

"Mum, you can't just hide problems in a syrup tin and think they're going to go away." Ray ran a hand through his hair, frustration mounting as the truth sank in.

"I'm sorry. It's just ... been hard. It's been a hard year."

"It's been a hard *life*. Yet, somehow, you and Dad have always persevered, and you've always been the people others look to for hope."

Mum stared at the letter. At least she wasn't crying. Ray wasn't sure he could handle tears right now. He absently thumbed through the remaining items in the tin but found nothing beyond various bills and receipts going back to the previous January.

Mum cleared her throat. "What happens now?"

How should I know? Ray wanted to shout. He'd never had to deal with this sort of thing, and he felt dumbstruck that Dad had left them in such a mess. He shook his head to clear his thoughts. Anger was not going to help.

"Did Dad have any life insurance?" Although it was probably pointless to ask.

Mum shook her head. "Just the church."

"What do you mean?"

"The funeral didn't cost us anything. The men got together to build the casket and dig your father's grave in the churchyard. Your aunts helped me dress him. The women all brought food and flowers from their own gardens—such as they were." Her voice cracked with emotion. "Doc said there'd be no charge on his end, and Pastor took care of the service."

Ray was grateful for the support of so many friends and family, but that wasn't what he meant. He couldn't count on the church to bail them out now. "Where did Dad keep important papers, like the mortgage?"

Mum rose and headed for the stairs. "There's a box under our bed. I'll get it."

Over the course of the next week, Ray learned enough about his father's business to understand where they stood. Even if they sold the animals, the farm equipment, and all their household goods, there would not be enough to meet the bank's demands.

Naturally. If their assets outweighed the debt, foreclosure would not be necessary. Uncle Henry helped him calculate acres of land with hopes they could at least keep the house and have a roof over their heads.

"But no one's buying. Not around here, anyway." Uncle Henry shook his head. "The bank knows that."

In the end, the bank allowed them to stay in the house for a small, monthly rental fee with the understanding the bank could sell it out from under them at any time. By seeding time, everything was gone—animals, equipment, the bit of feed they'd managed to store. The bank even took Dad's cantankerous old truck. Mum was allowed to keep a dozen chickens, but rather than eat the eggs, she let the hens nest with hopes of increasing her flock. Before that happened, her one and only rooster disappeared—likely, carried off by a fox or badger—and with him, her plan. Once again, Ray had failed to protect his family. Shame weighed on him, bowing his shoulders and head.

The bank left them with only essentials, taking Mum's china, silverware, and cameo brooch that had been passed down for generations. Nothing worth selling remained.

Nothing, except Ray's paintings. When the assessor didn't see any value in them, Ray loaded up every picture from the closet and the walls around the house except for the one of Sarah at the wishing well. That one would never be for sale—and certainly not to be made into a jigsaw puzzle.

On a sunny April Monday, he returned to Merry Times Amusements and sold all the paintings for seven dollars each. John Rawlings' jigsaw puzzle business was booming.

"I don't want you wasting your time delivering pictures, Ray." Mr. Rawlings handed him the cash. "Get home and crank out as many as you can, and let me come to you. People love your work, even the well-to-do folks. In fact, we've promised our loyal patrons a one-of-a-kind puzzle."

"One of a kind?"

"Instead of multiple copies of the same picture, we make only one and sell it at a premium. It's a prestige thing. The rich don't want to stoop to the level of those who do puzzles because it's the only entertainment they can afford. When they own a one-of-a-kind, it's like having a hoity-toity piece of artwork to brag about."

Ray nodded slowly, trying to grasp the inane workings of the human mind and heart.

"Of course, the unique ones have to be something special. You get busy now. Be sure to make 'em happy pictures with lots of color. That's what folks like."

They arranged a date for Mr. Rawlings to collect Ray's work, and he left with a nod to the smiling Miss Cook. At Eaton's department store, he purchased a supply of canvas and paint before catching his train home. Rawlings had offered to bring more when he came.

The living room became Ray's studio. With its south-facing window, it offered the best light and even a view—uninspiring though it was. Ray worked from sunrise to sundown to turn out as many paintings as possible, his production increasing each day along with the hours of daylight. It was as though all the images he'd ever envisioned floated to the surface, and Ray released them onto his canvas—horses, dogs, chickens, and cats. Pretty girls in pink frocks and boys playing ball at the Sunday school picnic.

He even painted a set of four pictures of the same plum tree, one for each season. The winter picture showed the barren tree still beautiful with a complete veil of hoar frost, surrounded by sparkling snow and a glowing pink sunrise. The second depicted it in full spring bloom, a glorious array of white blossoms like a bride ready for her wedding. In the third, the branches hung heavy with red plums and green leaves, carpeted by green grass.

In the last picture, the tree displayed a wild array of orange, red, yellow, and brown—with several plums lying among the fallen leaves below. Ray had such fun with this set, he lost all track of time as he poured his heart and soul into it. Caroline would often sit and watch him work when she got home from school.

After each picture dried, Ray carefully hung it in his bedroom. Filling the walls was the best way he knew to protect the paintings from damage without taking up space. It would also make them easy to display when Mr. Rawlings arrived.

True to his word, one mid-summer morning, a shiny, black Chevrolet pulled into the Matthews' yard, and John Rawlings stepped out, a roll of brown paper tucked under one arm. Ray went out to him, suddenly very aware of the peeling paint on the house and the deserted look of the farmyard. But the businessman didn't seem to notice.

"I'm in a hurry, Matthews. I'm hoping to get back to the city before the office closes for the day. Show me what you've got, and I'll be on my way."

On their path through the kitchen, Ray introduced Mr. Rawlings to Mum and Caroline.

"Would you like a cup of Ovaltine, Mr. Rawlings? I'm sorry we have no coffee."

"No, thank you, ma'am. Very kind of you, though."

Caroline stood drying her hands on a dish towel. "Hello, Mr. Rawlings."

"Nice to meet you, Caroline. Your brother should paint more pictures of you."

Caroline turned back to her work, but a blush crept up her neck.

"This way." Ray led Mr. Rawlings upstairs to his room and waved his arm around at the crowded gallery.

Rawlings stood in the center of the bedroom, slowly turning as he studied each painting. His face remained expressionless, but Ray detected a twinkle in the man's eyes. The work was at least as good as the first two batches he'd sold, now that he knew what made a good puzzle—lots of color and interesting detail.

"Excellent work, Matthews." This time, he actually smiled. "I'll take them all."

Ray grinned, his confidence soaring.

"And I already know which picture will be our one-of-a-kind. I bet you can guess."

Ray pointed to the four pictures of the plum tree. If he could sell all four together as a one-of-a-kind set, maybe he could earn four times the premium rate. "The trees? Four puzzles, one tree. You could promote it all kinds of ways. Folks could assemble one each season. Or you could put all the pieces together into one box for an extra challenge. You could even—"

Mr. Rawlings held up his hand. "The trees are great, but leave the marketing to the experts. Your job is to paint great pictures. Mine is to buy them and see that they get to the printing and cutting factory."

Ray had once asked to see how the puzzles were made, imagining rows of jigsaws manned by expert craftsmen in a large, noisy room near Mr. Rawlings' office. It had been disappointing to learn the pictures were sent to a plant in Minneapolis. Ray would have a long, expensive trip if he ever wanted to see it for himself. Despite his curiosity, watching his work be cut into small pieces would be too painful to watch. With each painting he completed, he had to remind himself why he was doing this—for Mum and Caroline.

Mr. Rawlings continued. "No, Ray, our winner jumped out at me the minute I stepped into the room." He took two steps toward the wall, leaned in for a closer look, and rested one finger on the portrait of Sarah. "This one right here."

Chapter Six

"Oh!" Ray made a move toward the painting, tripping on the braided rug and catching himself on the bedframe. "I'm so sorry. That one isn't for sale. I should have taken it down." He reached for the painting of Sarah.

Mr. Rawlings put a hand on Ray's arm. "Not for sale? It's your best one."

"It's..." Ray grappled for words. "I did that one years ago. I'm sorry. You can take all the others. I don't know what I was thinking, leaving it there." Ray couldn't bear to imagine Sarah's picture being chopped into pieces. "I can do another similar one for you. I just can't let you have this one."

"I'll offer fifteen for that one, seven for each of the others."

Ray's heart thundered in his chest. Why, oh why, hadn't he moved Sarah's portrait before the man came? It had hung on his wall so long, it felt like a permanent fixture. The thought had never even crossed his mind that Mr. Rawlings might want it—or become this determined to have it.

"No, sir. I'm sorry, but it's not for sale."

Mr. Rawlings crossed his arms and rocked back on his heels, studying Ray. "What if I said it was all or nothing?"

Was the man bluffing? How stubborn could Ray afford to be? If he let Rawlings leave empty-handed, he was stuck with a bunch of paintings and no way of selling them. No way of even recovering the cost of his supplies. More importantly, no way of paying the rent. He studied the picture of Sarah again. How could he even think of doing this to her?

That moment during his first visit to Mr. Rawlings' office surfaced. The man had been bluffing with his low-ball offer, and Ray had stood his ground. He'd risk it again, for Sarah.

"Then...I guess...it's nothing." Ray's hands trembled, but he forced himself to look the man in the eyes. "I've enjoyed working with you, Mr. Rawlings. But the painting is not for sale."

Mr. Rawlings frowned. "Cheeky one, aren't ya?" He heaved a great sigh. "All right. Fine. Keep your picture. Let's load up these others." He pulled out his wallet, counted out the cash while Ray watched, then handed it over. "I'll need five dollars of this back if you want the supplies I brought."

The deal made, Ray placed the remaining money in the top drawer of his dresser, and they took the pictures off the walls and wrapped them in the brown paper Mr. Rawlings provided. Mum and Caroline helped carry them down to the car, and the new supplies to the living room.

After they shook hands, Mr. Rawlings crawled in behind the steering wheel and rested an elbow on the window frame. "I'll be back in September if this crazy puzzle fad hasn't run its course by then. It'll happen eventually, you know. You'll be sorry you didn't sell that picture while you had the opportunity."

Ray put his hands in his pockets and shuffled one foot in the dust. "I'll take my chances, sir."

The man grinned. "I like your spunk, kid. You remind me of me." With that, he started the car and drove off.

Ray returned to his room and paused to smile at the painting of Sarah. "I won't let them do it, sweetheart," he whispered. "Never."

He pulled the money out of his dresser and carried it down to his mother. "Best if you take this to town while I get started on some new paintings." With the loss of the truck and horses, their only option was walking to town—a half hour each way.

"I was thinking the same. Thank you, Ray." His mother took the money. "This will take care of the rent through September and our bill at Sellinger's. I'll make something special for supper tonight. You're a good provider, son. Come on, Caroline. I know you want to come." She left the room.

Caroline lingered another moment. "I was listening from the stairwell when Mr. Rawlings was in your room." She creased her eyebrows. "You could have sold Sarah's picture for fifteen dollars."

Ray merely nodded. It must sound like a fortune to Caroline.

Her face relaxed. "I'm glad you didn't. You really loved her, didn't you?"

Still do. But he just ducked his head.

"Will you try to paint another one? Another portrait?"

"Maybe. But it won't be Sarah. I won't let them cut her up." He set a new piece of canvas on his easel. "I just can't. Maybe it's silly, but—"

"No. I don't think it's silly."

Ray smiled. "Thanks, sis. I'm not so sure Mum would agree. Better if she doesn't know."

"Our secret. Maybe you could do one of me that he would like just as much. With the wishing well, just like Sarah's picture, but me instead. I wouldn't mind being all cut up for a puzzle, not for fifteen dollars."

"Well, that's good, because they've already made one out of you."

Caroline's eyes grew round. "What?"

Ray laughed and raised his arms to fend off his sister's flailing hands as she came after him.

"I didn't even get to see it!"

TERRIE TODD

"Then you should be thrilled that it got cut up into five hundred pieces." Ray grabbed Caroline's wrists and held her until she quit squirming. "Am I right?"

"Quit your scuffling," Mum called from the kitchen. "Let's go, Caroline. You'll bring on another attack if you keep that up."

For all her protests, the gleam in Caroline's eye revealed she was flattered her portrait had sold. He watched through the window as the pair walked down the dusty lane and the farm grew quiet. Then he sat back to envision his next piece.

He had just finished covering the white canvas with a light coat of sky blue when a vehicle rumbled up their bumpy lane much too fast, its horn honking. Ray nearly dropped the paintbrush he was holding. *What on earth?* Setting the brush carefully on the edge of his palette, Ray ran to the door and threw it open. It was their neighbor, Eli Robinson.

"Ray!" Eli's head hung out the window as he pulled up in a cloud of dust. "Ray! Fire! We need all the help we can get!" Eli turned his truck around to face the road while he waited for Ray.

Not another one. The dryness of the last several years had made house and barn fires common, but there had not been one yet this year. Who would it be this time? Ray quickly covered his paints. He ran through the kitchen, grabbing a pair of leather work gloves and an empty bucket from beside the stove before he slammed the door behind him. When he got to Eli's truck, the passenger door hung open. Eli took off down the lane before Ray could pull it closed.

"Where is it?"

"It's the Martindales." Eli's voice was somber, and he gave Ray a knowing look.

Sarah's family.

"Let's go!" Ray thumped the dash. He tried not to think about Sarah's home in flames, her room scorched beyond recognition. It was the only home she'd known. She'd been the oldest, followed by five boys and then three little girls all in a row. The youngest was still a baby when Sarah died.

Smoke rose from the Martindale house as they approached, but no flames were visible. Two ragtag lines of men, women, and children—most of them Martindales, by the look of it—snaked from the well to the house. A steady stream of water buckets moved up and down the lines. Ray was out of the truck before it even stopped. He ran to the house, where a ladder rested against the north wall. From the top of the ladder, Sarah's father was handing buckets of water through the window to someone inside and tossing down empties so he could grab the next full one. Who was inside?

Mr. Martindale's face was pale, his hands shaking.

"Let me take over!" Ray hollered. He handed Mr. Martindale's bucket to the nearest person in the brigade while the man climbed down. Ray scrambled up the ladder, and Eli followed, taking a place at the halfway point. Smoke billowed so thickly from the windows, Ray couldn't tell who was inside. Suddenly, the sooty face of Sarah's brother Arnie was in front of him, flinging down an empty bucket to his brothers below and taking a full one from Ray. Water sloshed over the side as they made the exchange.

"Arnie! You need to get out of the smoke!" Ray turned to take another full bucket from Eli. "Can you get down the stairs? Let me take your place!"

Arnie reappeared, handing him another bucket. "We've almost got it. A couple more buckets full just to make sure it's out."

Just as Ray turned to grab the next full bucket, his foot slipped on the wet rung. He scrambled to catch himself, grabbing for the windowsill. He missed. His body hurtled downward, taking Eli with him and sending the ladder on a sideways trajectory.

Ray and Eli landed in a heap on the ground, now muddy from the water. He was vaguely aware of someone catching the falling ladder and righting it. Someone scrambled to the top to keep the bucket brigade going. Eli jumped to his feet and held out a hand to help Ray up.

But Ray couldn't move. Flat on his back, he fought to draw another breath.

"You all right?" Eli bent closer to Ray's face. "C'mon, buddy. I broke your fall, and I'm okay."

Suddenly, Sarah's mother was there, on her hands and knees in the mud beside him. "Ray? Can you hear me?"

He heard her perfectly, but he couldn't seem to respond.

"He's had the wind knocked out of him," she shouted. "Give him some room. Eli, help me roll him onto his side."

Mrs. Martindale and Eli rolled Ray onto his right side, and two things happened simultaneously. He took a massive gulp of air, and the worst pain ever stabbed through him. Something was wrong with his right arm. As soon as the others took their hands off him, he flopped back over to get the weight off his arm.

"You all right, Ray?" Mrs. Martindale stroked the side of his face.

"Fine. I'm fine. Take care of your family. Where's Arnie?"

She looked around. "He's out of the house. Everyone's fine. The fire's out." She ran a hand through his hair and put her face closer to his. In a soft voice, she added, "and *you're* family too." She helped Ray pull himself to a seated position. "You just rest there awhile."

After she moved away and the group's attention returned to the house, Ray tried to assess his injuries. The pain in his arm was so excruciating, he might pass out if he tried to stand. Even worse, he felt like the biggest idiot. Instead of coming to the aid of the Martindales, he'd only managed to prove his own ineptitude once again and draw attention to himself in the process. When would he ever become something other than the sissy artist who couldn't pull his weight with the other men?

People continued milling in and out of Ray's line of vision as he fought to stay conscious through the blinding pain. Mr. Martindale announced that the danger was over and thanked everyone for coming. Gradually, the crowd dispersed. The younger Martindale children went home with their cousins, while the older ones waited for instructions from their parents. Everyone looked dazed.

Eli stood in front of Ray. "Ready to go?" He held his right hand out to help Ray up, but Ray's right arm wouldn't move. "Give me your other hand."

With their left hands clasped, Ray rose to his feet. A gasp escaped his throat as he let go of Eli and clutched his right arm.

"C'mon. You're all right. Let's get you to the truck."

Eli was speaking softly, and Ray knew what he was trying to do. Neither of them wanted to give the Martindales anything more to worry about. He managed to walk to the truck, and they both climbed inside.

"It's broken, isn't it?" Eli started up the truck.

"I don't know. It just hurts like everything."

"Off to see Doc, then." Eli turned in the direction of town as Ray's head slumped against the back of the seat and his surroundings faded to black.

Chapter Seven

"Ray, I'm real sorry." Eli stood from his seat in the doctor's waiting room and shook his head as he frowned at the bright white cast on Ray's right arm. "I'd never have made you come if I'd known how this was going to turn out." He opened the door, and Ray walked out into the waning afternoon daylight where Eli's truck waited.

"No need to apologize—how could you have known? It's my own fault for trying to be a hero." Ray allowed Eli to close the truck door behind him.

"I'll take you home. What did Doc say?"

Ray looked down at his cast and tried to wiggle his fingers. The pain made him wince. "Broken in two places. I'll have to wear this at least six weeks." He held up a bottle of pills with his good hand. "And take these for a while."

They rode in silence a moment, then Eli asked the obvious. "So, uh... you going to be able to paint?"

Ray sighed. "I really don't have much choice. Not unless I can figure out another way to earn some money."

When they pulled into the yard, Mum and Caroline rushed out of the house. "Is the fire out? Is everyone okay?"

News must have reached them while they were still in town. Ray and Eli both climbed down from the truck.

When Mum saw the cast on Ray's arm, her mouth dropped open. "What in the world—?" She hastened to assist Ray up the porch steps and onto the bench.

"Mum, it's okay. I broke my arm, not my leg. I can walk just fine."

Eli leaned against the railing. "Well, maybe not just fine. You're still a bit shaky, bud. Might want to take it easy the rest of the day."

"Thanks for bringing him home, Eli. Are the Martindales all right?"

"Yes, ma'am. The fire was pretty much under control when we got there, I think." Eli removed his hat, slapped it against his leg, then returned it to his head. "They all got out. I can't say how much damage there was to the house, though. I'll swing 'round there before I go home and find out what they need."

Mum followed Eli to his truck, and their conversation gradually faded out of Ray's earshot.

"Does it hurt bad?" Caroline plopped down beside Ray.

"A bit." The dread in his stomach hurt worse. How would he ever produce a dozen new paintings to sell Mr. Rawlings when he returned in September?

Eli drove away, and his mother turned slowly back to the house.

"I want to hear all about it, but first, you need to peel out of those smoky, muddy clothes." She nodded toward Ray's pants. "Leave 'em out here, and get yourself cleaned up. Caroline, you come with me and set the supper table while I fill a washbasin for your brother."

Ray hadn't even realized he was caked in mud. "Peeling off" his clothes was a lot easier said than done with one hand. He worked up a sweat just struggling to get his pants off. The shirt was even trickier, though the right half had been draped loosely over his shoulder. Finally down to his undershorts, he headed straight for the washbasin just inside the back door. Hot water, soap, and a ragged old towel waited for him. Scrubbing himself clean offered another reminder of how much he normally depended on both hands. Between the frustrating challenge of performing this simple task, the pain still throbbing in his arm, and the worry about the future, Ray gritted his teeth.

He leaned toward the small, foggy mirror hanging crookedly above the basin and inspected a bump on his forehead. He tried to pull some hair down over the red lump but soon gave up and turned toward the clean clothes Mum had placed on a chair. It took five times longer than usual, but he managed to work his way into the trousers and white undershirt. Looking at the clean pair of socks, he opted to go barefoot rather than put forth the effort required to get them on his feet.

Over a supper of fried egg sandwiches, Mum and Caroline listened intently to his story. Ray tried to gloss over his own embarrassment at having fallen off the ladder, focusing instead on Arnie's heroics as he stayed inside the burning house until he made sure the fire was out.

"You shouldn't have gone." Mum made the statement as if it were a fact.

"Shouldn't have gone? That wasn't an option." He worked at cutting a bruised spot out of his apple one-handed, but it was hopeless. "That's not how you and Dad raised me. What if it had been *our* house? Wouldn't you want every able-bodied man within ten miles to help?"

She looked at him and let out a sigh. "You're different from the other men."

"Different?" He gave up on the knife and bit into the apple. Better to keep his mouth full of food than say something he'd regret. Even Caroline was quiet.

Mum began clearing her own dishes. "I just meant..."

Ray worked his way around the apple's core, and Mum still hadn't completed her sentence. He finished it for her.

"You just meant what? I'm a delicate artist? Not fit to carry my fair share of the weight?" He rose from his chair and took his plate to the dishpan.

"No!" Mum picked up the kettle from the stove and poured hot water into the dishpan. "I'm just saying you can't take such risks. You *need* your hands—"

"I don't need my hands any more than any other man needs his. And the Martindales need their home."

He stomped toward the living room and surveyed his "studio" from the arched doorway. With a heavy sigh, he sat in front of the canvas he'd abandoned that afternoon. He studied it a moment, then picked up a brush with his left hand. What had one of his professors said? The skill is in the brain, not the hand. It's in the heart. He'd shown Ray and his classmates paintings done by people holding a paintbrush in their mouths and even their feet. If they could do it, surely, he could too. He still had a hand.

But the longer he worked, the more he struggled. The lines on the canvas were shaky. The picture in his mind refused to transfer through his left arm. He tried in vain to hold the brush between the tips of his right fingers, standing to position himself in a way that he could brush some paint onto the canvas, even swinging his entire body when the pain in his arm became too great. But it was hopeless. As soon as he wiggled his fingers, pain shot up through his arm, and he sank to the chair again as the objects in the room swirled around him. He closed his eyes to make the spinning stop.

He jumped when Caroline's voice broke his concentration. "Why don't you try again tomorrow? It's been a long day."

Ray turned toward her. "How long you been standing there watching me?"

Instead of answering, she approached. "I'll help you clean this up." She took the brush from his hand and placed it in the jar of paint thinner, then picked up the cleaning rag he kept handy and wiped a spot of paint from his fingers.

"You shouldn't be breathing those fumes." Ray ran his left hand through his hair. Caroline's lungs had done surprisingly well lately, even with all the dryness and dust. But why push their luck?

"I'm all right." She studied Ray's face a moment, then glanced out the window where Mum was emptying water from the dishpan onto a row of tomato plants. "Mum didn't mean it. Not like you think."

"I know how she sees me. I'm not like Dad—we all know that."

"Doesn't make you any less of a man. She's just scared."

He let out a big sigh and slumped against the back of the chair, watching his little sister clean up his supplies.

"You should go get some sleep." Caroline capped the tube. "You're as white as this paint."

"That's *frost*," he muttered. "Not white."

"Go to bed before I frost *you!*" She whacked him on his thigh with the rag.

Exhausted, he climbed the stairs one at a time instead of his usual manner of skipping every other one. The painting of Sarah greeted him, and he thought again about her family who had already lost so much. "I couldn't even help save your home, sweetheart," he whispered. "They'd have been better off if I hadn't shown up. I'm just a useless, clumsy ... *artist*. Maybe you dodged a bullet when you went to Heaven instead of marrying me."

Too weary to face the frustration of undressing, Ray flopped onto the bed and stayed on top of the covers. Between the pain in his arm, the worry in his mind, and the ache in his heart, he spent a long, fitful night tossing from his back onto his left side and back again. Somehow, he had to figure out a way to support his family. Should he even try to keep painting, or would he only waste precious time? Was there another way he could bring in some income? Should he return to the city and look for work there? But what could he do with his dominant arm in a cast and sling?

What do I do, Sarah? What should I do?

But the answers didn't come.

Chapter Eight

September arrived, and with it, a letter from Mr. Rawlings. He would arrive on the fifteenth and eagerly anticipated seeing Ray's new paintings. He assured Ray he was prepared to buy a dozen if they were the quality he needed. In other words, if they were at least as good as the last batch.

Ray surveyed the eight pictures he'd managed to paint left-handed. He hated them all. Mum and Caroline had propped them around the floors and furniture of the studio-living room, encouraging him and insisting the pictures were just fine.

"They don't look like your work, it's true," Mum said. "But that doesn't mean they're not good."

"It's like he's getting two artists for the price of one," Caroline chimed in. "He'd be stupid not to take these."

But Ray's eye was keener. A child could have done these. Mr. Rawlings had rejected finer work than this by other artists, but these paintings were Ray's only hope. He'd have to convince the man to buy them, or his family wouldn't make September's rent. Mr. Sellinger had warned Mum there'd be no more credit on groceries until they cleared the current balance. And, after studying his latest x-ray, Doc had insisted on leaving Ray's cast on another week.

"Those were bad breaks, Ray," the doctor had told him. "They're fusing, but slowly. And you're still going to have to go easy with that arm once the cast is off. The muscles will be weak."

On September fourteenth, another dust storm blew through, and Caroline responded with another wheezing episode. While Ray covered his paintings with old sheets to protect them from the dust seeping in around window frames, Mum tended to Caroline upstairs. How many thousands of times had she squeezed the rubber bulb of that glass nebulizer, trying to get the epinephrine to his sister's ailing lungs? Ray could hear Caroline's labored breathing from the main floor and wished more than anything he could take away her struggles once and for all.

"Ray." Mum stood at the top of the stairs, her face pale. She clutched an empty medicine bottle in her hand. "We've used it all, and she's not getting better. Can you fetch the doc?"

Ray ran all the way to town, his arm throbbing. His heart plummeted when the nurse told him Doc was assisting an urgent home baby delivery. He left a message about Caroline's situation and headed to the drugstore.

"I always keep a supply of epinephrine on hand with your sister in mind, Raymond." The druggist nodded, then dipped his head. "But unfortunately, it didn't come in this week. I'm not sure what's going on, but the company is low on the supply. I'll telephone over to the store in New Haven, but even if they have some, it'll be tomorrow at the earliest before we can get it here."

Ray pressed the man for something—anything—to help his sister.

"I can't prescribe, Ray." He shook his head and shrugged one shoulder. "Only dispense. There's an over-the-counter product you could try, although I seem to recall your mother taking this home before and not having much luck with it." He led Ray to a shelf and pulled down a blue bottle with a creamy-looking liquid inside. "You know," he added slowly, "I read an article about kids with breathing issues like your sister's. They say it's a nervous problem. That a child's wheeze is a suppressed cry for her mother. That it's a form of depression. But then, who isn't depressed these days, eh?"

Ray took the bottle. "My sister receives plenty of love and attention from her mother. Can you add this to our account, please?"

The druggist sighed. "You and every other customer."

"My art buyer is coming tomorrow." Ray signed his name in an awkward scrawl on the receipt. "I can come in and square up with you then, and hopefully pick up the other medicine at the same time."

The man waved him off with one hand and reached for his ledger with the other. "Go. I hope it works for her."

But it did nothing. Caroline's horrible rasping continued through the night while Ray frantically worked to finish one more picture and their exhausted mother did everything in her power to ease his sister's breathing. The gasping and coughing provided a constant backdrop for Ray's creativity, resulting in a dark and depressing story on his canvas. Not the sort of thing puzzlers wanted to assemble when they were grasping for a little joy in their dreary lives.

He finally gave up and went to sit with Caroline so Mum could get some sleep.

Barney's barking competed with Caroline's coughing when a car pulled into the yard at ten the next morning. Ray went out to greet Mr. Rawlings, and before the man even emerged from his car, his eyes clamped on Ray's arm.

"What happened here?" He nodded toward the cast.

"Little accident." Ray shrugged. "Firefighting for a neighbor. Cast should be coming off in a week."

Mr. Rawlings studied Ray's face. "Has it kept you awake at night? You look awful."

"My sister's not well." Ray led the man into the house.

He need not have explained, for Caroline's coughs and wheezes could be heard from the moment they entered the kitchen.

"You folks need to get electricity out here." Mr. Rawlings removed his hat but hung onto it. "I hear they've got electric apparatuses now for lung troubles. You been able to paint with that thing on your arm?"

"Yes, sir. I've got eight pictures ready to go." Ray led the man into the living room where he'd uncovered the new paintings. His heart raced as he stood back.

Mr. Rawlings stood still, taking in the paintings all at once. Slowly, he shook his head, then he let out a heavy sigh. "You should have telephoned."

"Sir?" Ray pretended not to understand.

Mr. Rawlings raised his voice and slowed his speech as though speaking to a child. "You should have found a phone and called me about your broken arm. I've wasted an entire morning and a precious tank of fuel coming here for nothing. I'm sorry, Matthews. I can't use any of these."

Ray's legs felt like jelly, but he resisted sinking into a chair. "Are you sure?" He walked over to the picture of a country cottage, the best of the lot. "See how the light shines out from the window of the cottage here? People eat that up."

"My six-year-old grandson could have painted that."

Ray had no answer. The only sound was Caroline's horrific coughing.

"I don't appreciate my time being wasted." Mr. Rawlings returned his hat to his head. "How long until you can paint me a dozen good ones, with your right hand?"

First, the cast needed to come off, and he had no idea how much painting he'd be able to do until the muscles strengthened. A dozen paintings? It could easily be Christmas. By then, his family would be out of a home. Ray's stomach churned.

He spoke with as much confidence as he could muster. "By the first of November."

"You know there *is* a way you can save this from being a totally useless day." Mr. Rawlings raised his pointer finger. "My offer still stands on that painting upstairs."

Ray met the man's gaze, then turned to look out the window. Barney lifted a leg on one of Mr. Rawling's tires.

"It's still up there, isn't it?"

Ray swallowed back whatever was trying to escape his stomach. "Yes, sir."

"Well?"

No. There were some things a man didn't budge on. He'd just gathered the courage and the words of denial when someone cleared their throat softly, and he looked over his shoulder. Mum stood in the doorway. Had she heard the whole conversation?

Mr. Rawlings turned toward the door. "Oh, Mrs. Matthews! Sorry about your troubles. I hope your daughter gets well soon. Nasty cough, that. It's not TB, is it?"

"No." The dark circles under her eyes and the weariness in her voice broke Ray's heart.

Mr. Rawlings put his hat on. "Well, unless you can talk your son into selling me that painting of the girl by the wishing well, I have no further business here today." He headed for the door.

Ray followed, trying to avoid Mum's imploring gaze.

"Ray, please..." she whispered. She looked so worn and thin, a breeze could blow her over. Another heavy wheeze from upstairs punctuated her plea and drew her attention.

"Mr. Rawlings, wait!" The cry burst from Ray's lips.

The man paused but kept one hand on the door handle.

"I'll sell you the painting on two conditions."

Rawlings waited, unblinking.

"You'll use it as one of your unique puzzles. No duplicates."

"I told you that in the beginning, didn't I? Premium price for you, prestige for some rich customer. Everybody wins. What's the second condition?"

"That you not reveal my name." Ray couldn't bear this ultimate treachery, laying Sarah's memory on the altar of amusement to be pulled apart.

Mr. Rawlings raised his eyebrows. "Bold move. Could add some intrigue to the project. I'm glad you finally came to your senses."

Ray swallowed hard. "Wait here."

He took the steps two at a time before he had a chance to change his mind. He charged straight into his bedroom and, without pausing, gently lifted the portrait of Sarah from the wall. Gazing at the face he had loved with all his heart, he gripped the frame.

"I'm so sorry, Sarah. You know I didn't want this."

It's only a picture, Ray. You're being ridiculous. You can paint another.

The thought had come before. Sometimes it was Mum's voice, sometimes Mr. Rawlings'. Sometimes it was Sarah herself. Still, the idea of her portrait being cut into five hundred or even a thousand pieces—being put together and taken apart over and over—felt like the worst sort of sacrilege. He would never paint another picture of Sarah. Time would erase her face from his mind's eye, and he wouldn't have the heart for it, anyway. Perhaps it was time to let go.

"I'm sorry," he whispered again. Then, as though he somehow held the power to jinx the picture or to prophesy, he added one more thing. "May the puzzle never be fully assembled until you and I are reunited, my love."

Part 2: 1953
Danny

Chapter Nine

*D*anny Gordon ran all the way home from school, his unclipped galoshes flapping against his shins in a crazy rhythm. Classes were out for a full two weeks for Christmas. That morning, Mum had let him and Reggie unwrap the present Grandma and Grandpa Gordon sent from Saskatoon. It was always a jigsaw puzzle, and every year, they began it on the first day of Christmas holidays. His mother would have the pieces laid out on a folding table in the living room, ready to begin work.

It wasn't that Danny enjoyed assembling puzzles all that much. He'd much rather be outside, throwing snowballs or building a snow fort with his buddies. Rushing home meant he could beat his little brother at his own game—stealing a piece from the puzzle. Reggie was only eleven, but he'd figured out early that if he could sneak a piece before anyone noticed and keep it in his pocket, he'd be guaranteed the chance to put in the last piece to complete the picture—even if he hadn't contributed much effort. It wasn't fair. Danny and his mother did most of the work.

On Christmas Day, they'd get a lot of help when the aunts, uncles, and cousins came over, along with Granny Cook. They worked in shifts of three or four people, trading places as they got bored or someone's eyes grew too weary to continue. Sometimes, they'd finish the puzzle that evening—all but the last piece. Then

Reggie would come strutting along like Granny's prize rooster and say, "Oh, is this the piece you're all looking for?"

Danny wanted to throttle him. The grownups just laughed and thought Reggie cute. The cousins held mixed opinions. The girls, especially the older ones, found Reggie adorable no matter what stunt he pulled. The boys, for the most part, tolerated him. Last year, Danny had caught Reggie slipping the puzzle piece into his pocket and had tried to teach him a lesson. But after washing Reggie's face with snow and threatening to pound him to a pulp if he didn't turn over the piece, Danny only got himself in trouble. When Reggie went crying into the house like a big baby, Mum sentenced Danny to work.

"If you have so much energy to spare, you can chop that pile of wood." Mum had stood in the doorway, hands on her hips. "Come on, now. Get to it!"

That night, the family had cheered when Reggie plopped the last piece of the puzzle into place to complete a picture—ironically—of a dozen children playing in the snow.

This year, Danny would be the first to swipe a piece, and he'd hang onto it as long as necessary. No matter what his bratty little brother did, Danny could hold out longer.

He entered the dark kitchen. "Mum?" He dropped his school bag and slipped out of his boots, leaving them dripping on the little mat inside the door. A note lay on the kitchen table.

Danny,

I got called in to work and didn't want to miss the chance to earn a little extra. Should be home by eight. We can start the puzzle then. There's leftover soup in the icebox for supper. Mum.

P.S. Reggie: Listen to your brother!

Danny's heart sank. So many times, he wished his mother stayed at home like his friends' mothers.

"They have husbands who work hard to provide for the family," Mum had explained three years earlier when Danny complained about having to stay at Granny Cook's house after school. "You know lots of other daddies died in the war, not just yours. We're not the only ones in this predicament, so we mustn't feel sorry for ourselves."

Danny was two and his mother still carrying Reggie inside her when the news came. In the years since, she'd shown the boys photographs of their father. She told Danny stories, trying to trigger a memory he might hold deep inside somewhere. Did he remember a tall, dark-haired man holding him on his lap in church? Grasping his hands as he learned to walk? Sharing a slice of bread? Danny only shook his head.

"Billy Fingerson's dad died in the war, too," ten-year-old Danny had argued. "He has a new one now. You could get a new dad for me."

His mother sighed. "It's not that simple, sweetheart."

Now thirteen, Danny understood more about how men and women fell in love and all that romantic stuff. Being the man of the house had its perks, like bossing Reggie around when Mum wasn't home. But at times like this, life would be nicer if Mum didn't have to work at all, let alone two jobs. She worked most of the week at a diner and sometimes got called to fill shifts at a garment factory. He loved coming home to find her here. The house would be filled with the fragrance of home-baked bread or stew simmering on the stove. Patti Page or Eddie Fisher would be crooning Mum's favorite tunes from the radio on the kitchen counter. Or, this time of year, Christmas carols.

Danny flicked the radio on and hung up his coat. Sure enough, "Hark, the Herald Angels Sing" played. He turned on some lights, then wandered to the living room and plugged in the multi-colored lights on the Christmas tree. Somehow, the urgency of beating Reggie to the jigsaw puzzle had passed. He hadn't really taken a good look at the puzzle box that morning. It still lay on the table unopened. The picture on the front seemed awfully girlish—a young lady peering into a wishing well with flowers all around. Grandma and Grandpa Gordon must have chosen one that would appeal to their daughter-in-law more than their grandsons this year. Fair enough. They had assembled their share of cars, trucks, and wildlife scenes. Mum had always been a good sport about that.

Scuffling sounds came from the back steps. Reggie charged inside and started hollering before he even had the door closed. "Didja open it yet?"

"No. Close the door—you're letting all the cold air in," Danny called back from the living room.

"Where's Mum?" Reggie stuck his head into the room and looked around.

"Working."

"Oh." His little brother's face registered the same disappointment Danny had felt when he read the note. "'Til when?"

"Eight o'clock, probably."

"Can we open it?"

"She said to wait."

Reggie sighed. "Wanna eat supper now?"

"It's only four o'clock, dufus."

"So? I'm hungry. And what difference does it make? Mom's not going to know if we eat at four o'clock or seven o'clock or somewhere in between."

He had a point. Danny's stomach growled too. Why not eat their supper? Besides, they were on Christmas vacation. If they couldn't start their puzzle, they needed to find some way to celebrate.

Reggie picked up the puzzle box and gave it a shake. As long as the box remained sealed shut, his brother couldn't sneak a piece. Danny went back to the kitchen and pulled Mum's vegetable soup from the icebox, then dumped it into a pan and lit the stove. "Wash your hands." he instructed Reggie.

"You didn't wash yours."

"Don't need to. They're clean."

"Are not."

"Are too."

The arguing escalated into a chase, which quickly escalated into dishtowel snapping.

"Ow! That hurt!" Reggie yelled when the towel smacked his bare arm.

"Big baby."

Reggie grabbed another towel, twirled it tight, and attempted to snap him back. To Danny's horror, the towel hit the handle of the pot on the stove, knocking it to the floor. Hot soup splattered everywhere—all down the front of the stove, onto the cupboards, the table and chairs, and mostly on the floor. The pot lay upside down in a puddle of soup on the black-and-white tiles.

"Now look what you did!"

"You started it!" Reggie scowled back. "Besides, you're in charge. What are we going to eat now?"

"Quit worrying about your gosh-darn stomach, and let's get this cleaned up."

"Not me. You're the one in charge. You clean it up."

"You're helping me, Reggie, or so help me, I'll tell Mum everything."

It took the boys a half hour to clean up the mess, and by that time, their stomachs were really rumbling. Danny got out a loaf of bread and placed it on the table with two butter knives and the peanut butter jar. He hated the job of stirring up the peanut butter to mix the oil in and wanted Reggie to do it while he cut the bread. But sure as anything, the clumsy little mutt would slop peanut oil everywhere, and they'd be right back where they started with a worse mess to clean up. Plus, the peanut butter would be dry and ruined for as long as the jar lasted. Danny stirred it himself, then sliced the loaf.

They went through eight slices of bread and four glasses of milk.

Reggie spoke around a mouthful. "You should learn to cook for real."

"Cooking's for girls, dumbo."

"Don't call me dumbo. And lots of men cook. They're called *chefs*. And they make gobs of money." Reggie licked a smear of peanut butter from his thumb.

"How would you know anything about it?"

"I know lots."

"Do not."

"Do too."

It was only when their arguing ceased that they noticed a strange silence in the house.

"The radio." Danny turned to Mum's pride and joy. "How come it's not on?"

"How should I know?"

Danny walked over to the kitchen counter to examine the radio. Broth and small chunks of vegetables lay on top and trailed down the sides to puddle on the counter. His heart sank. "Oh no."

"What?" Reggie joined him.

"You wrecked Mum's radio. Look."

They continued to argue over whose fault it was while they tried to clean up the radio. Danny found a screwdriver to take it apart. He poked around inside for over an hour and reassembled it, but it still wouldn't play.

"You're in big trouble now, Reggie." He carefully pushed the radio back into place. "I can't fix it."

"Me? You started it."

Danny didn't have the energy to revisit that old circus again. He could picture Mum's disappointment when she couldn't listen to the radio anymore and prayed a silent prayer that it would somehow, miraculously, work next time she turned it on.

They'd each settled into an armchair with comic books when Mum walked in the door.

"Merry Christmas!" she called out. "Did you know it's snowing?"

He and Reggie ran to the window to look out. Snow had been sparse so far this winter, and a good snowfall would give them plenty to do in the next few days. Once the sidewalk was shoveled, of course. Mum always made them do that first, then they were free to play.

"Did you save me any soup?" Mum hung up her coat and filled the tea kettle.

Danny and Reggie looked at each other.

"Uh...sorry, Mum." Danny didn't take his eyes off Reggie's. "We were just so hungry."

"And that was just such good soup," Reggie added.

Danny scowled at him.

"What?" Reggie whispered. "I didn't lie."

"No matter," Mum said. "I'll make myself a sand—oh, my goodness! You *must* have been hungry! There's only a scrap of bread left." With a sigh, she found some cheese and sat down at the table to eat it with the remaining crust of bread. "I can bake more tomorrow."

The boys told her about their day while she ate, then the three of them moved to the living room.

Mum put her teacup on the puzzle table. "Bring the lamp over here, Danny."

Danny unplugged the floor lamp from its spot in the corner and brought it over to the folding table, then plugged it in and turned it on. Mum took a seat and picked up the puzzle box.

"Oh." She sounded shocked. "Oh, my."

"What?" Reggie stood beside Mum while Danny sat, waiting for her to unseal the box.

"See here?" Mum pointed to a seal in the corner of the lid. "This means it's a unique puzzle. And it's old—probably fifteen or twenty years, yet it's never been opened."

Reggie practically pressed his nose to the box. "What's 'you-neek' mean?"

"Unique. It's a one-of-a-kind. They were making these as specialty items when I worked for Merry Times Amusements during the Depression. They were expensive. I wonder how your grandparents ever got a hold of this one. When they call us on Christmas Day, I'll ask."

"Why did nobody open it?" Danny rested his chin in his hands.

"I don't know, but I suspect whoever bought it wanted to keep it sealed, thinking it would increase in value."

"What do you suppose it's worth?" Danny took the box from Mum and examined it more closely.

"Oh, I doubt it increased. Probably just the opposite."

Reggie slumped into the third chair with a sigh. "So are we gonna open it or what?"

Chapter Ten

anny watched Mum's face expectantly.

"Of course, we're going to open it. Grandma and Grandpa Gordon sent it for us to enjoy, and that's exactly what we're going to do." She turned to Danny. "Please bring my paring knife."

Danny fetched the knife from the kitchen. He had only seen his father's parents a handful of times, but they wrote letters every month and sent gifts at Christmas and birthdays. At Mum's insistence, Danny and Reggie made thank-you cards from her stash of construction paper. She would tuck them in with her own long letters and school pictures, keeping her in-laws abreast of the boys' grades and school activities.

Grandma's return letters, without fail, would mention how much Danny resembled his father. She'd even sent a picture of Daniel, senior, at the age of ten. Mum kept it side-by-side with Danny's Grade Five school picture on the kitchen bulletin board. He glanced up at the photos now. Everyone who saw them remarked that they could be the same person.

Danny couldn't see it.

"Thank you, son." Mum took the knife and carefully cut along the edge of the box until the seal was broken all the way around. Then she lifted the cover off and propped it against the wall on the tabletop for reference. Together, they spread all the pieces out, flipping them right-side-up. They were different from those in any puzzle Danny had ever done—made from very thin wood instead of cardboard.

"Cool." Reggie examined a piece.

"Go put on a sweater if you're too cool." Mum didn't bother to look up until Reggie started giggling. "What's so funny? If you're chilly, grab a sweater."

But Reggie only laughed harder.

"It's the latest slang," Danny explained. "He means the puzzle pieces are cool—you know, interesting."

"Well, wherever did you learn such a silly thing? Just say what you mean."

Danny flipped over more pieces. "Didn't you have slang words when you were growing up?"

Mum grinned. "Oh, sure. But ours made sense."

"Like what?" Reggie sat up straighter.

"Well…instead of *cool*, we might have called something *snazzy*. Or *keen*. Or *swell*."

Reggie snorted. "Swell."

"You still use those words all the time," Danny pointed out. "They're not really slang."

"Well, not anymore. Now they're just ordinary words. But when I was a kid, they were new. That's how our vocabulary grows."

"Does that mean everybody will be saying 'cool' when we're old like you?" Reggie asked.

"Probably, if it sticks. Some words do, some don't. And guess what? If it sticks, it won't be 'cool' to say it anymore." The lamp light erased the worry lines and made Mum's pretty smile the focal point of her face. Her eyes danced when she looked at the two of them. On an evening like this, you wouldn't know she was a lonely widow.

By the time they had the outside edge assembled, it was nearly bedtime.

"Okay, boys. Pajamas on. I'll make some cocoa."

Danny passed Reggie on the stairs and got to their bedroom first. The bunkbeds in one corner had been a gift from Granny Cook two years ago, a gift which had thrilled Danny. He'd watched the double bed they'd shared being hauled away, then scrambled up to the top bunk and claimed it as his own private space, never to be trespassed upon. That night, nine-year-old Reggie had climbed the ladder to snuggle up to Danny, who promptly told him to scram. But his little brother stayed on the top bunk that first night despite Danny's protests. Thankfully, darkness hid the grin he couldn't seem to wipe away as they fell asleep.

After the first night, Reggie remained in his own bunk.

Shivering, the boys scrambled into their pajamas, bathrobes, and slippers as fast as they could. When Reggie hung his trousers over the back of the chair, Danny picked them up and dug his hand into each pocket.

"What are you doing?" Reggie tried in vain to grab the pants.

Danny's search, however, unearthed only one marble, a jaw breaker, and a bit of lint.

"Checking for puzzle pieces." Danny picked up Reggie's shirt from the floor and searched the chest pocket. Nothing.

"You may as well give up." Reggie shrugged. "I've outgrown it."

Danny gave the shirt a shake for good measure before he dropped it on the floor. "I doubt it."

When they returned to the kitchen, Mum was pouring hot cocoa into three mugs. "You boys have any idea why the radio isn't working?"

"Not me." Reggie lied. "Maybe Danny knows."

Mum looked at Danny. He shrugged and went over to the radio. He turned it on, fiddled with the tuner and the volume dial, then tapped the side. Nothing. A lot of good his prayer did. "Maybe it'll work again tomorrow." *Once all the soup dries.*

"Can we drink this in the living room?" Reggie took his first slurp of cocoa.

"Yes. Careful now."

They settled onto the couch, one boy on either side of Mum, where they got the best view of the tree. Mum had turned off the lamp over the puzzle table so that only the glow of the Christmas lights illuminated the room.

"You boys remember what the Christmas lights symbolize?"

Danny did, but he let Reggie answer. "Jesus is the light of the world."

"That's right. Let's remember that Christmas isn't all about getting presents. It's about God loving us so much he sent his son to earth to save us from our sins."

Danny swallowed his cocoa, but his deception niggled at him. "Do you have to work tomorrow?"

"Yes. But I'll be off by four, and then we can attend the Christmas Eve service."

Mum began humming "Silent Night." Danny and Reggie stared at the tree, sipped their cocoa, and allowed the old carol to settle them. Danny swallowed his guilt about the radio and asked Mum for a story.

"What about?"

"Tell us about when you worked for the puzzle company."

Mum smiled. "Well, it was during the Depression, like I said before. I was fresh out of high school, and jobs were scarce. But a man named Mr. John Rawlings was a friend of my father's. Your grandfather convinced Mr. Rawlings to hire me as his secretary-receptionist, and I worked there for two years, until I married your daddy."

"Did you get to see them make the puzzles?" Reggie drained his cup, tapping on the bottom.

"You know, I never did. Mr. Rawlings' job was to find and buy paintings that would make good puzzles. Then they were sent off to a factory in Minneapolis and shipped out from there. He sought out art students, mostly. People with real talent and promise but who were desperate for cash. I always felt a bit sorry for them."

"Do you remember when he bought this one?" Danny moved to the partially completed puzzle on the table and picked up the lid, turning on the lamp.

"Let's have a closer look." Mum took the lid and turned it this way and that. "It's dated 1939. I was gone by then. That September, Canada joined the war, and life changed for everyone."

She studied the picture of the young lady at the wishing well more closely. "This work does remind me of a certain artist, though. I can't remember his name. I wonder why it's not on here. We always made sure the artist got credit on the box, if not on the puzzle itself. That's strange."

"Who do you think painted it?"

"Well, if it's the young man I'm thinking of... oh, what *was* his name? Nice fellow. Awfully insecure, but he was probably the most talented of all the artists Mr. Rawlings bought from. Although Mr. Rawlings would never tell him that, of course. Didn't want him selling to our competition or making demands. His puzzles were popular, too. He would have got a good price for this one, being a one-of-a kind."

"Enough to make him rich?" Reggie's face lit up.

"Not rich enough to never have to work again, if that's what you mean. If anyone got rich from the puzzle business, it was Mr. Rawlings."

Danny studied the picture. "I wonder who the lady is."

"Me, too," Mum said softly. "She's lovely, whoever she is. You boys can work on it some more tomorrow while I'm at the diner, and hopefully, we'll finish it on Christmas Day with your cousins. Then you can tell Grandma and Grandpa Gordon thank you when they call, and we'll find out what they can tell us about it. Now let's all get some sleep. Up the stairs with you both. I'll be in to say good night in a bit."

Danny was in that delightful, dozy space between awake and asleep when Mum came into their room. She leaned down to kiss Reggie and whisper good night, then straightened up to do the same with Danny. She ran a hand gently over his hair. "My big boy," she whispered. "Sleep well."

Danny rolled over and drifted off. That night, his dreams were filled with images of colorful Christmas lights, busted radios, a handsome man in a soldier's uniform, and a beautiful young lady peering down a wishing well.

Chapter Eleven

*D*anny and Reggie spent December twenty-fourth shoveling snow and playing in it, then working on the jigsaw puzzle while Mum was at work. They attended church together in the evening, lighting candles and singing carols. Afterward, they were invited to their neighbor's house for eggnog. When they finally came home, there'd been no more time to work on the puzzle.

On Christmas morning, Danny woke to the annoying urgency of Reggie's scratchy voice right beside his ear.

"Get up! C'mon, Danny, wake up. It's Christmas!"

Danny opened his eyes just enough to see it was still dark. "Go away, it's not even light yet." He rolled over, his back to Reggie. If he was honest with himself, he was every bit as curious as Reggie about what they might find under the tree. But he couldn't give his brother the satisfaction. After all, Danny was thirteen. Everybody knew teenagers preferred to sleep late.

"It's nearly six o'clock!" Reggie grabbed Danny's quilt and yanked it off. "C'mon, let's go downstairs."

Danny flailed an arm in Reggie's direction but didn't manage to make contact. He pulled the covers under his chin and curled up without a word.

"Fine, then. I'm going without you." Reggie left the room.

Danny threw the covers off and dashed after him, catching up at the end of the hallway and passing him on the stairs. The tree lights glowed, and Mum bustled around the kitchen in her bathrobe. Under the tree sat four brightly wrapped presents that hadn't been there the night before. On the table, the jigsaw puzzle lay about one-quarter complete.

"Morning, boys. Merry Christmas!" Mum stood in the kitchen door, both hands curled around a coffee cup and her hair all fuzzy around her face. "Turkey is stuffed and in the oven. Shall we have breakfast first or open presents first? As if I don't know the answer."

"Presents!" Reggie was already under the tree and had figured out which gifts were his.

Mum laughed and took a seat on the sofa, turning on a lamp and placing her cup on the coffee table. "All right. See those two that look the same? You need to open them first, at the same time."

Reggie handed Danny a package with his name on it while he ripped into an identical one. Danny followed suit, knowing full well it would be something to wear. Sure enough, they both held up a new pair of pajamas. Danny had never mastered the feeling of gratitude for new clothes, especially pajamas, even though Mum worked hard to teach them how to express it. At least his didn't match Reggie's. Danny's were red-and-black plaid—far more mature than Reggie's cowboys and horses, and for that, he could be grateful.

"Thanks, Mum. These will be nice and warm."

Reggie parroted him. "Thanks, Mum. I like the cowboys." He made lasso motions over his head.

"Well, the ones you're wearing are getting awfully short. You're both getting so tall."

Danny looked down at his pajama bottoms, noticing for the first time how much ankle stuck out beneath them. He had, however, noticed that he now stood eye-to-eye with his mother.

"Can I open this one?" Reggie had grabbed his next gift and was shaking it.

Mum chuckled. "Yes, but don't shake it too hard. It might be breakable."

Reggie tore the wrapping paper away to reveal a colorful box labeled *Mr. Potato Head.*

"I knew it!" Reggie yelled. "Mum, can I have a potato?"

Mum laughed and pulled an almost perfectly round potato from the pocket of her bathrobe. "I had a feeling you might be asking."

Reggie opened the box to find plastic hands, feet, ears, two mouths, two pairs of eyes, four noses, three hats, eyeglasses, a pipe, and eight felt pieces resembling facial hair. Each had a push pin on the back by which you could stick it into a potato—or any vegetable—to create different characters. Reggie went to work while Danny watched with a grin.

"You know," Mum picked up the box and studied it. "This toy is a symbol of prosperity and better times. When I was a child, we wouldn't dare waste food to make a toy. And during the war years, this toy would have been considered unpatriotic. Food was rationed."

"Thanks, Mum. It's just what I wanted." Reggie didn't bother to look up but began rearranging Mr. Potato Head's features.

"Your turn, Danny." Mum picked up the remaining gift and held it toward him.

Danny's gift was in a box too. Unlike Reggie, he carefully peeled back the tape so Mum could reuse the wrapping paper. He lifted it away to reveal a Chinese checkers game.

"Hey, thanks!" Definitely more interesting than new pajamas. He'd have to recruit Reggie if he wanted to play the game, but that was all right. His brother would do until his cousins arrived.

"Now those marbles will get lost awfully easily," Mum warned. "You'll need to be diligent about putting everything away. A game's no fun if parts are missing."

"I know." Danny opened the box and examined the board and playing pieces, then closed it up again and pushed it aside for later. Reggie had designed a Mr. Potato Head he was satisfied with and stood it on its feet on the coffee table. Mom seemed to be enjoying just watching them. The house felt eerily quiet without the radio providing background music, and he knew Mum missed it.

A new thought occurred to Danny. There were no gifts for Mum. Why had he never noticed that before? Did she care? She didn't seem to, sitting there watching her boys. But surely, other mothers received Christmas presents, didn't they?

He looked under the tree just in case something had been missed. But if neither he nor Reggie bought their mother a gift, who would? Danny had stopped believing in Santa Claus long ago, if he ever truly had. It was not something Mum had ever played up.

"There's no gift for you," he said softly.

Mum smiled. "My gift is watching you boys enjoy yours. Besides, the puzzle was just as much for me as for you fellas. Maybe more."

Reggie piped up in a cheerful tone. "I'll betcha Granny Cook will have a present for you when she gets here."

"I'll bet you're right. Let's go see about breakfast, shall we?"

Shortly after noon, the house filled with extended family. Danny set up the Chinese checkers on his bedroom floor where Reggie and the older cousins joined him. That left the little ones—one baby and two toddlers—downstairs with the adults who gathered around the jigsaw puzzle. They worked in shifts, chasing children and visiting, cooking and setting the table. So much noise filled the house, no one seemed to notice that no Christmas carols were playing.

Except Danny.

When they were called down for dinner, more gifts crowded the space under the tree. After filling their stomachs with turkey and all the trimmings, the family squeezed into the living room. The puzzle was now at least three-quarters finished, and Danny eyed Reggie. Had the little rotter stolen a piece yet, or was he finally growing up as he claimed?

Their uncle read the Christmas story from Luke chapter two in Mum's Bible. Then they opened gifts, starting with the youngest child. Granny Cook had bought and wrapped books for everyone. Most were used but each carefully selected to suit the age and interests of the recipient.

"Cool!" Danny grinned when he opened not one, but two Hardy Boys books he hadn't read—*The Wailing Siren Mystery* and *The Secret of Wildcat Swamp*. He studied the covers. "Thank you, Granny!"

Granny smiled back. "Now, no reading under the covers with a flashlight. It's hard on the eyes." Then, with a twinkle in her own, she added, "Why do you think *I'm* half blind?"

"He'll have those read before school starts again." Mum held up the book she had just unwrapped, a hardcover copy of *The Silver Chalice* by Thomas B. Costain. "You might even enjoy reading mine when I'm done with it, Danny. Thanks, Mother."

After the gifts, most of the kids went upstairs to play. Danny joined his uncle and mother at the puzzle table, where they kept working until only one hole remained near the center.

"Looks like Reggie's done it again." Danny sighed.

His little brother hovered near the kitchen door, sucking on a candy cane and watching the progress of the puzzle.

"Well, Reggie? Where is it?" their uncle asked. "Get over here and finish this thing, or I'll have to come tickle it out of you."

"Actually…" Mom pointed. "We need *two* more pieces, not just one."

His uncle studied the hole more closely. "Look at that. So we do. How'd he manage to steal two pieces that go together?" The two of them began checking the floor under the table.

"Did you take two, Reggie?" Mum frowned. "You know this is becoming less funny every time you do it, right?"

"No, Mum." Reggie took another lick of his candy cane. "I can honestly say I did not take two."

Danny fumed. The piece he had so carefully sneaked into his dresser drawer two days before now burned a hole in his pocket, and he had no doubt Reggie had one in his too. No way was he going to be the first to give in.

"C'mon, Reg," Granny coaxed.

"Oh, just forget it. He only wants attention." Danny walked away from the table. Maybe if no one cared, Reggie would realize how stupid his game was and finally grow up. Yet the question nagged at him—if it was so childish, why had Danny participated, and why was he so determined to hold out? To teach that little rotter a lesson, that's why. "I'd rather play Chinese checkers, anyway."

Danny headed up the stairs. As he neared the top, he peeked back down. The adults moved casually away from the puzzle to the sofa and armchair. If they cared about the missing pieces, they did a good job of hiding it.

"He wants us to make a big deal of it," Mum confided to his aunt in a low tone that nevertheless reached Danny's ears. "But I won't give him the satisfaction."

Aunty sniffed. "I should think you could bring his little tradition to a swift end with a swift swat to his *hind* end."

"I'm choosing my battles." Mum spoke through clenched teeth. "This is not one of them."

Danny spent the remainder of the evening playing games with his cousins until it was time for them to leave. They said their goodbyes in the kitchen.

When the house grew quiet again, Mum placed a long-distance phone call to his grandparents in Saskatoon. Danny could hear her end of the conversation.

"However did you come by this puzzle? ... No, I don't. ... Really? ... I don't know, I suppose someone thought it would be more valuable unopened. ... Yes, we finished it tonight, and it's beautiful."

Mum was fibbing to her in-laws so they wouldn't be disappointed about the missing pieces. Or, to be specific, their bratty grandson. Grand*sons*. Mum would never suspect Danny of stooping to Reggie's trick. She would assume her youngest had taken two pieces, for whatever reason, and she would remain determined not to make a big deal of it.

When it was his turn to talk to his grandparents, Danny thanked them for the puzzle and told them about his other gifts and his plans for the next week. Reggie did the same, and they ended the call.

"What did Grandma have to say about the puzzle?" Danny asked his mother.

"She said they bought it at an estate auction, along with another that they sent to Uncle Rick's family." Uncle Rick was his father's brother. He and Aunt Melva had three daughters and lived in Calgary. Danny had seen them only a couple of times. "And guess what? When I called Grandma, she had just gotten off the phone with Uncle Rick. Turns out she sent them the puzzle meant for us and vice versa, by mistake."

"I *knew* it was a girlie puzzle." Reggie flapped his arms in the air, his wrists limp.

Danny pondered this. "I wonder what theirs was like."

"She said it was a campfire scene of some sort." Mom grinned. "I'm kind of glad they got mixed up. This one's beautiful. Or it will be, as soon as we find those pieces and finish it." She gave Reggie a knowing look.

Danny spent the rest of his Christmas holidays reading his new books, shoveling snow for two neighbors who paid him fifty cents each, and building an impressive snow fort with a buddy up the street. Mum returned to work, leaving Danny in charge. He dutifully made sure he and Reggie did their chores, ate a reasonable lunch, and cleaned up the kitchen after themselves. Every time they walked past the puzzle table, the hole in the middle of the wishing well seemed to grow larger. Nobody said a word about it.

On New Year's Day, they helped Mum take down the Christmas tree and haul it to the backyard. As they boxed up balls and tinsel and the delicate angel that always graced the top, Mum reminded them to keep a lookout for the missing puzzle pieces. Afterward, she hauled out her Hoover and vacuumed the whole house. No puzzle piece materialized, and neither of her stubborn sons said a word. That night, they were in bed by eight-thirty. They'd stayed up until midnight the night before, and school started the next day.

Another week went by. Once or twice, Danny was tempted to put his piece into the puzzle. Then he'd remember Reggie's sickening satisfaction when he'd waltz in with the last piece as though it was some kind of trophy. He couldn't stand the thought. He wouldn't give in.

On Friday when they came downstairs for breakfast, the puzzle table was missing. The armchair sat in that space as usual, and there was no sign of the girl at the wishing well.

"Where's the puzzle?" Reggie called from the middle of the living room.

Danny side-checked him as he walked past into the kitchen.

Mum stood at the stove, stirring oatmeal. She didn't bother looking up. "In its box. On the closet shelf with the others."

"But it wasn't finished!" Reggie whined like a baby.

"And I guess it won't be. I want my living room back." Mum plopped oatmeal into two bowls and set them on the table. "Eat up."

That afternoon when he returned home from school, Danny went to the hall closet and found the box with the wishing well puzzle on top of the stack. Checking over his shoulder, he carefully lifted the lid and tossed in the piece he'd been carrying around in his pocket.

He hoped his little brother had the decency to do the same.

Chapter Twelve

Another snowstorm dumped three inches on them a week or so later. After Danny and Reggie finished clearing their own steps and sidewalk, Danny bundled up to go knock on a few doors to offer his services.

"Go find your own customers," he told Reggie when his little brother wanted to tag along and help.

To Danny's chagrin, Reggie did just that. By the end of the day, they'd both earned three dollars.

Now they walked the aisles of the Woolworth's store, gaping at endless rows of games, comic books, BB guns, lunar rockets, view masters, roller skates, and musical instruments. With each item Danny picked up and imagined taking home, the vision of Mum's smiling face as she watched her sons open their Christmas presents rose to mind. And with it, the silence of the radio she had so loved.

He put a guitar back on the shelf and watched Reggie, who held something called a "space cadet signal siren" flashlight in one hand and a paint-by-number box in the other.

"Reg," he said, "Mum's birthday is in two days. We need to replace her radio."

Reggie looked up with a wrinkled brow. He took a quick breath, but for some miraculous reason, he didn't argue. He slowly laid the toys back on the shelf. "Where are the radios?"

The boys located the electronics aisle. Shiny, new, tabletop radios encased in varying colors of plastic sat on display, any one of which would make Mum smile. And all of which cost more money than they had.

"These are twenty dollars!" Reggie's eyes looked like they might pop out of his head. "Why don't we get her a nice apron or something, and that way, we'll still have money left over for—"

"Reg. An apron? You've seen how she misses her radio. She tries turning the old one on at least three times a day, and it never works." Danny ran his hand along the smooth surface of a beautiful red radio with a big, white tuning dial and matching white volume button.

"Maybe we can get the old one fixed."

"Mum tried that already. The guy at the repair shop said it's so old, he can't even find the parts it needs." He sighed. "And I'm pretty sure Mum knows we had something to do with why it doesn't work anymore, even though she doesn't let on."

Guilt pierced Danny's chest. Their aunt always said things such as, "You're too easy on those boys, Margaret. Just because they don't have a father doesn't mean you can let them off easy. You're not doing them any favors."

Mum always defended her sons. But maybe she shouldn't.

Reggie sighed. "Well, we don't have enough money, and we can't earn enough by her birthday. Even if we get another big dump of snow tonight." He fiddled with the tuning dials. "Maybe we could sell something."

"Like what? We don't have anything anybody wants."

"Mom said that jigsaw puzzle Grandma and Grandpa Gordon sent was valuable—a one-of-a-kind." Reggie turned the *on* button on one of the radios until it clicked. Nothing happened.

A salesman approached. "Can I help you boys?"

"This radio doesn't work." Reggie clicked the dial off and on again.

The man studied him over the top of his glasses. "I can assure you, all of these radios are in perfect operating condition. They work just fine once you plug them in."

"Oh." Reggie dropped his gaze to his shoes, a half grin on his face.

Straightening his spine, Danny tried to rise to the same height as the salesman. "We're in the market for a new radio. These are a bit steep. Do you have anything in the six-dollar range?"

The man looked Danny up and down. "No. You might try the pawn shop across the street." Pushing his glasses up, he turned to help another customer.

The air in Salty's Pawn Shop hung heavy with musty, stale air. Shelves placed ridiculously close together spilled over with every imaginable item. What didn't fit on the shelves lined the floor along each wall. A row of radios in varying degrees of age and condition filled one shelf, all at varying and cock-eyed angles to make them fit. Reggie even found a television set. "Hey, let's save up and get Mum a Tee-Vee!"

Danny scowled at him. None of their friends had televisions, and he'd overheard Mum say, "It will be a cold day in you-know-where before I'll allow such a time-waster in my home."

"We don't even have enough money for a used radio, you goose. How could we ever pay for a TV?"

Reggie wandered back to Danny's side and eyeballed the radios. A nine-dollar price tag hung from the cheapest—one which had clearly seen better days. Reggie tapped the surface of a newer model, its aqua-blue casing polished to a shine. "Mom would love this one."

Danny checked the tag. Ten dollars. He could picture the radio sitting on the kitchen counter in place of the old one. Reggie was right. Mum would love it. It even matched the curtains she'd sewn last summer, the ones she'd hung with pride on the window over the sink and tied back with bands made from the same fabric.

"You boys just gonna gawk all day?" Rail-thin and in need of a haircut, the proprietor wandered over.

Reggie piped up. "Do you buy jigsaw puzzles? Because we got a real valuable, one-of-a-kind one."

Danny turned to stare at his brother.

The pawn man evaluated Reggie. "A unique puzzle?"

"That's right. Unique. And it's old too. Nearly as old as our mother!" Reggie's boldness grew in proportion to the value of the puzzle. "Betcha it's worth twice what these radios are."

The man chuckled. "I doubt that, but I might take a look at it. Can you guarantee me it's not missing any pieces?"

"Yes, sir! We'll run home and get it right now if you promise not to sell this radio while we're gone."

Before Danny could wrap his mind around what was happening, he and his brother were hustling down the sidewalk toward home. "We can't just take the puzzle without telling Mum," he protested.

"Why not? She's not going to miss it. Especially once she gets her new radio."

"But you heard the man. How can we guarantee him it's not missing any pieces?" Danny had to run to keep up with his wiry little brother. "Remember? It was missing *two* at Christmas."

Reggie stopped short. He looked Danny straight in the eye. "Did you put *your* piece back?"

Danny stared at him. Without breaking eye contact, he slowly nodded.

"Then trust me. I know for a fact all the pieces are there." He took off again. "C'mon."

At the house, Danny pulled the puzzle off the shelf. He gazed at the pretty girl with the flowers in her hair. "I dunno about this, Reg. It's not exactly ours to sell. Grandma and Grandpa gave it to all three of us."

"That makes me and you two-thirds owners. We have a madority."

"Majority. And it hardly counts if Mum doesn't even know we're voting."

Reggie grabbed the puzzle and headed for the door. "Do you wanna give Mum that beautiful blue radio for her birthday, or do you wanna hang onto a girlie puzzle that will only sit in the closet? C'mon."

Danny pictured the surprise on Mum's face when she opened her gift. The empty spot on the kitchen counter mocked him. The radio really would look perfect against the yellow walls. With a sigh, he followed Reggie out the door and back to the pawn shop.

Two days later, the three of them sat at the Saturday morning breakfast table polishing off bowls of cornflakes and toast. Mum kept unusually quiet while Reggie chattered on about his plans for the day. As soon as he mentioned one of his buddies was coming over to shoot marbles, Danny waited for Mum's caution—*no playing for keeps!* She always insisted their friends return home with all the marbles they'd brought, which pretty much defeated the whole purpose of playing.

But today, Mum said nothing. Was she blue about her birthday? She probably assumed they'd forgotten—and maybe everyone else too. He caught Reggie's eye and raised one eyebrow. Their signal. Reggie raised both eyebrows back. Reg had thought supper would be the best time to surprise their mother, but Danny figured she would have a better day if she could listen to the radio all day. He nodded, and Reggie slipped out of his chair and dashed upstairs.

"Where's he off to in such a rush?" Mum asked. "Reggie! You didn't ask to be excused!"

"It's okay, Mum. He's coming back." Danny grinned. "We got you a little something."

Now it was Mum's turn to raise her eyebrows. "You did?"

"Uh-huh."

Reggie thundered back down the stairs. He walked into the kitchen with a big smile on his face, holding a present wrapped in flowery paper and tied with a pink ribbon. Danny started singing "Happy Birthday," and Reggie chimed in. He placed the gift beside Mum's plate and stood there until the song ended. Mum smiled through it.

She held one hand over her heart. "I can't believe you boys remembered. What is this?"

"Open it!" Reggie returned to his own seat.

Mum untied the ribbon and carefully removed the paper to reveal the beautiful blue radio. "Oh, my goodness! How did you boys—?"

"Do you like it?"

"Like it? I love it! But wherever did you get it? How could you afford it?" Mum ran one hand over the surface and gently fingered the dial. Then she looked at Danny. Then Reggie. "I know you boys were shoveling a lot of snow, but I never dreamed—"

"It isn't brand new," Danny explained. He avoided Reggie's eyes, hoping his little brother knew better than to offer more information. "But it works."

"It's beautiful. Thank you so much. I have the two most thoughtful sons in the whole world." She reached out both hands and stroked Danny's right cheek and Reggie's left. "You boys have made my day."

"Are you going to put it where the old one used to sit?" Danny bounced over to the counter. "We thought it would look real pretty with your curtains and all."

Mum looked around the room. "You're right, it would. But you know what? The repair man told me the old radio got moisture inside, and a kitchen counter might not be the best place to keep one." She stood and carried it over to the little corner stand below the bulletin board and telephone. Clearing off space, she set the radio on the top shelf and plugged it in. In seconds, she had tuned in to her favorite station and was soon swaying to the Tokens crooning "The Lion Sleeps Tonight."

Five years later, when Danny left home to start college, it was that aqua blue radio that captured his attention as he took one last look around his mother's kitchen. Though the curtains at the window had faded, they still matched. The radio still worked. And to his knowledge, the puzzle with the girl at the wishing well had never been missed.

Chapter Thirteen

Wishing Well, Manitoba. July 1953

Caroline Watson pulled the last of the shirts from the clothesline and dropped them into her basket with a tired sigh. She paused to arch her back, hands on hips, as she counted small blond heads for the umpteenth time that day. Eight-year-old Nate sat on the back step, not-so-patiently teaching his six-year-old brother how to tie his shoes. The girls played in the sandbox, two-year-old Pearl's blonde curls reflecting the sun. Caroline took in the peaceful scene, knowing full well some sort of crisis was only moments away. It always was with this crew.

If Mum could see me now. Caroline swatted at a mosquito on her arm before picking up her laundry basket and heading for the house. *Four children in ten years and another on the way.* The health problems that had so plagued her growing years and convinced her mother that Caroline wouldn't live to adulthood, let alone marry and bear children, had resolved. The only remaining traces came on an occasional spring day when the air was rife with pollen. Even then, it was too minor to hold her down. *Thank you, God, for restoring my life* had become a daily prayer. She never wanted to take her health or breath for granted.

By the time Caroline reached the back step, Nate's patience with his little brother had dissolved, and they were squabbling.

"Not like that!" He let out a frustrated growl.

"It's all right, Nate." Caroline dropped the basket on the top step. "I'll take over from here. Thank you for helping your brother. Why don't you see if you can find that rubber ball that went under the front porch yesterday?"

She sat on the step and turned her attention to her younger son's shoes while Nate scampered around the corner to the front of the house. When she looked up again, he was dashing back.

"Mum, Uncle Ray is here!"

Ray? Caroline hadn't seen her brother in weeks.

Nate disappeared again, no doubt rushing to greet his uncle. Caroline followed him around the corner with the girls. Sure enough, her brother was closing the door of his beat-up truck and ruffling Nate's hair.

"Hey, there, Scooter."

From the day Nate was born and named after his grandfather, Ray had nicknamed him *Scooter*. Caroline had a hunch her brother couldn't bring himself to say their father's name.

"Ray! This is a surprise."

"Hi, Sis. Thought I'd stop by and see these rascals before they grow up and move outta the house. Looks like this one's ready to pack up any day." He poked Nate's ribs as the boy laughed and darted away, then scurried back for more.

"Not me. I'm not movin' out. Never!" Nate circled around Ray.

"You say that *now*," Ray teased. "And who are these beauties?"

Caroline scooped Pearl up to ride on her hip, and the little girl promptly popped a thumb into her mouth. Her sister leaned into Caroline's skirt, hanging onto the hem. Caroline gently pulled the pudgy hand away from Pearl's face and examined it for dirt. "Say hello to Uncle Ray."

"'Lo, Unca Way." The little girl's soft voice could barely be heard.

Ray leaned in. "Hi there, Pearl. Where's that other brother of yours? I don't see enough people here." He made a great show of counting the three children. "One, two, three...somebody's missing. Who is it?"

Both girls pointed chubby fingers toward the back of the house, then Pearl stuck her thumb back in her mouth.

"He's learnin' to tie his shoes," Nate volunteered. "I already know how."

"Well, we need to find him, because your ol' Uncle Ray's got peppermints burnin' a hole in his pocket, and they're not coming out until I see all four of your faces."

Like a jack rabbit, Nate took off to alert his brother.

Caroline picked up her basket. "I'll make us some coffee."

Ray stayed in the backyard with the children while Caroline went inside to start her percolator. She pulled out some of the peanut butter cookies she'd baked the day before and arranged them on a plate. From the window, she saw her brother doling out peppermints and sitting beside Nate on the step to watch a shoe-tying demonstration. Two-year-old Pearl warmed up to Ray and climbed into his lap. When all four children had shown their uncle an empty mouth—their candy having been crunched up and safely swallowed—he set Pearl gently on the ground and began chasing the boys around the yard.

A lump formed in Caroline's throat. Ray would have made a wonderful father. Instead, he'd spent twenty years pining for his dead sweetheart to the point where Caroline had come to hate the memory of Sarah Martindale. She'd been only ten years old when Sarah died and hardly remembered the girl who had completely captured her brother's heart. Now forty, Ray remained alone on Mum and Dad's farm. Thanks to the Veteran's Land Act, Ray had been able to buy back enough fields to eke out a living after fighting for king and country in Italy. But he'd abandoned his art, and he'd abandoned God. He never showed his face at church and had expressed zero interest in meeting another woman. He'd seen more than his share of loss and had no desire to commit himself to another person he could lose. *Thank you, Lord, that he has at least allowed himself to love his nieces and nephews.*

She was pouring coffee into two cups when Ray came in the back door, carrying Pearl. "Those monkeys sure have energy. I'm pert-near worn out." He set Pearl down and washed his hands at the kitchen sink. "Coffee smells great."

"It's all poured." Caroline lowered herself into a chair where she could keep an eye on the backyard and stirred some cream into her coffee. What on earth had brought Ray by today? Would he feel pressured if she asked?

"How's that brother-in-law of mine?" Ray sat and took a big swallow of coffee, black.

"Much too busy." Roger Watson, Caroline's husband of ten years, worked as a carpenter in a booming economy. Even little Wishing Well had seen numerous new houses go up since the war ended. Roger had branched out on his own two years ago. "The new bank's nearly finished, and he's got a contract for an addition to the school."

"Well, you're doing your part to make sure that school stays full." Ray sipped and chuckled. "When's this one coming?"

"Three more months. Mid-October."

"Right around Mum's birthday?"

Caroline had thought of that too. "Yes. Wouldn't that be something if it was born on Mum's birthday?"

Ray smiled, his blue eyes focused on her face. "She'd be so proud. All these kids. You, lookin' so healthy."

Caroline could feel the tears welling up. "You sacrificed a lot for Mum and me, Ray."

He waved his hand to silence her. "Aww—"

"No, I mean it. I don't want you to think I don't appreciate everything. I wish there was something I could do in return."

"Oh yeah? Like what?"

Caroline could think of several things. She'd love to see her brother spruce himself up a bit. A new wardrobe would be a great start, though she dare not say so. He probably couldn't afford it. Maybe the day would come when she and Roger could help Ray out financially.

She couldn't say all that, though. "Oh...I don't know. Just...pay you back somehow. There must be something you need."

Ray shrugged. "Don't be silly."

The two of them sat silently for a moment, watching Pearl make a mess of a peanut butter cookie. Finally, Ray cleared his throat.

"I've had some news."

Caroline waited.

"The town council approved Sarah's wishing well."

Caroline stared at him. *Wishing well?* She hadn't thought of the wishing well project in years. "I didn't know that was still...in the works."

"Well...I think you know, I've been setting money aside for it. And finally—"

"Wait a minute." Caroline shook her head. "*You're* funding this?"

Ray nodded.

"*Completely?*"

"That's why it's taken so long."

"Are you going to be on the hook for its upkeep too?"

Ray frowned. "I agreed to maintain it, yes. It's going to be a wonderful addition to our little town square, and ultimately—a memorial worthy of Sarah. It's what she always wanted."

"Ray." Caroline swallowed, trying to slow down her response and grant her brother some dignity. But this was ridiculous. "She's been gone twenty years."

"Twenty-one."

Pearl had begun to fuss. Caroline picked her up, crossing to the sink to clean the little girl's hands and face. "Right. Twenty-one years. That's a long time. With all due respect, you need to let her go and get on with your life. You know she would have wanted that for you—"

"I *have* gotten on with my life. I went to war, Sis. I survived when lots of other fellows didn't. Now I'm getting on with my life. Again."

"*Are* you? When's the last time you went on a date?"

"A date? Who on earth would I—"

"Your last date was with Sarah, wasn't it?"

Ray slapped his hat across his knee and returned it to his head. "So what if it was? Maybe I have no interest in other—"

"You're alone. You don't have to be."

Ray turned his gaze out the window. "Maybe I like it this way."

They stayed silent while Caroline settled Pearl at a child-sized table with crayons and paper. With a sigh, she returned to her seat across from her brother. "How much is this wishing well costing you?"

Ray stood and headed for the door. "I don't see how that's any of your business. I came here to share my good news, and I thought you'd be happy. I should have known better."

"Ray, wait! I'm sorry." Caroline followed him and stood in the doorway. "Don't go. I shouldn't have said that. Come back and tell me about the well."

But Ray kept going.

"You leavin', Uncle Ray?" Nate called out from the sandbox.

Ray just waved his hand and disappeared around the corner of the house. Caroline heard the engine start and the truck's wheels crunch against gravel as he pulled out onto the road.

Oh, God. Forgive me. How long would it take for her brother to confide in her again?

Part 3: 1975
Felicity

Chapter Fourteen

Winnipeg

Felicity Cooper could feel sweat trickling down her back and pooling above her belt as she entered Principal Connery's office.

"Have a seat, Miss Cooper."

She sat in one of the chairs across from her boss. A cigarette smoldered from an overflowing ashtray on his desk.

"I don't mean to pry into your personal life," he began. "But when it affects your students, I'm afraid I must."

Felicity didn't need to ask what he was talking about. The day before, she had fallen asleep at her desk while her pupils wrote a test.

"I'm sorry, Mr. Connery. I just—I had a rough night with my mother. I won't let it happen again."

The principal narrowed his eyes. "You won't let what happen again?"

Felicity's eyes darted from her boss to the window and back again. "Falling asleep in class. Isn't that what you wanted to see me about?"

The man stared, making Felicity want to disappear. "I'll have to add that to the list."

He had a list? She scanned the surface of the principal's desk. He pulled out a drawer to his right and removed a file folder. He opened it, adjusted his glasses, and focused on the top sheet of paper.

"September twenty-third, nineteen seventy-four. Terry Johnson's mother called to say you returned Terry Dickson's essay to her son in error."

"Oh, yes. I remember. That was just a silly mistake, and I corrected the mix-up—"

"She said it was the third time he'd come home with another student's work."

It's not my fault every third baby was named Terry *fifteen years ago.*

Without looking up, he kept reading. "October fourteenth. One of your colleagues found you in their classroom prepared to begin a class you weren't scheduled to teach."

"Oh, yes, that was—"

"November eleventh. You called me at home to say you wouldn't be in. I reminded you it was a school holiday—Remembrance Day."

"I know I've been a bit scatter-brained, Mr. Connery—"

"And I know you've been run ragged, looking after your mother."

Felicity sighed. Mama's signs of dementia had begun when Felicity was in her early twenties and engaged to be married. But her fiancé's big dreams did not involve staying in Winnipeg. When it came down to following him to Vancouver or staying behind to care for her mother, Felicity chose Mama. Last she'd heard of the man, he was the divorced father of three children—confirmation she'd made the right decision.

Mr. Connery returned to his sheet. "At Christmas time, your class had nothing prepared for the concert—*nothing!*—even though your class has always been the most prepared other years. In January, I received three phone calls from parents saying their children couldn't understand their math assignments. Three *different* parents. And since then, there have been complaints about chaos in your classroom, students not being challenged while others are over-challenged. And you've already been late twice this week. It's only Wednesday."

"Sir, I can do better. I just need to—"

"I know you can, because you have in the past. You need to make some alternate arrangements for your mother, Miss Cooper. You are burned out. I bet you have no social life, do you?"

"Not really. No, sir." Felicity couldn't remember the last time she'd spent any time with a friend. Or even alone, for that matter. Her biggest outing, church on Sunday with her mother, was turning into a far bigger burden than blessing in the struggle to get herself and Mama both ready.

"Do you have a sibling who could help you?"

"No. It's just me." Three years earlier, Felicity had let her apartment go and moved back into her mother's house—a good solution until Mama was no longer safe during the day while Felicity taught school. After a few near misses, Home Care provided some relief. But over the past year, work became a respite. She dreaded returning home, hearing from the nurse how her mother's confusion continued to accelerate.

Mr. Connery gave her a sympathetic look. "I want you to succeed here, Miss Cooper. You've been a wonderful teacher until the last year or two and I am convinced you're simply wrung out from caring for your mother. It's understandable. And it's commendable. But it cannot continue, not like this." He slid a brochure across the desk toward her and tapped it with one finger. "My father lives here, at Sunny Grove. My sister tells me it's a good facility, that Dad is doing well. Maybe you could get your mother on their wait-list."

Why had he based his recommendation on his sister's word? The home was right here in Winnipeg. Had he even visited his father? But she was in no position to challenge him. He was right. Her professionalism had been slipping—more than slipping.

"I'd hate to see your own health suffer." The principal made a note at the bottom of the sheet of paper and returned it to its folder, tapping it on his desk. "Keep the brochure. I can't tell you what to do, but I need to see some serious improvement by the end of the school year if we're to renew your contract."

Their conversation led to a visit to Sunny Grove, a panel's assessment of her mother, three interviews, one home visit, and a three-month wait. Sickening, waiting for someone to die so that her mother could have a place at the care home and Felicity could return to her own life. But the relief on the day she received the phone call overrode all other feelings.

Until the day she moved her mother in.

"This is a lovely room, Mama. Isn't it?" Felicity opened the curtains wide and turned to face her mother, who sat quietly on the single bed. "You'll get lots of sunshine...once it decides to shine."

"Where is this place?" Mama's gaze shifted in slow motion from the family photos Felicity had arranged on the dresser to the lamp on the nightstand.

"It's the Sunny Grove care home. Remember? We've been talking about this for months. Today's the big day! Here you are in your new home."

Mama stared back as though hearing the words for the first time. "Where is this place?"

"In Winnipeg. Just a twenty-minute drive from our house." Felicity moved away from the window and walked around the room. "See, we brought your favorite chair and afghan. Here's your Bible and your slippers. You've got your own bathroom, and I've put all your toiletries out for you."

"Why am I here?" Her voice sounded like a small, frightened child's.

Felicity sighed. At thirty-two, wasn't she much too young to be dealing with this?

"Mama, you're here because it isn't safe for you to stay at home anymore."

"Where is this place?" her mother asked again.

"It's just a few blocks from home. Why don't we see how your TV comes in?" She walked to the small black-and-white set she'd brought from Mama's bedroom at home and turned it on. "You can watch all your favorite shows here just like you did at home. Isn't that great?" She adjusted the rabbit ears and twisted the channel selector until a familiar soap opera filled the screen. "Today's Tuesday, so you can watch Mary Tyler Moore this evening. And I'll come watch *The Waltons* with you on Sunday night, same as always."

Mama stared blankly at the television.

"C'mon, let's move you to the chair so you'll be more comfortable."

Felicity helped Mama settle, and she cooperated without a word. She was generally easy during the day. It was nighttime that had proven difficult. Felicity hadn't had a good night's sleep in months. If she wasn't coaxing Mama back to bed following a sleep-walking incident, she was lying awake listening for the click of her bedroom door. Felicity had finally taken the home care nurse's advice and installed a lock on the door. But the one night she'd locked Mama in with hopes of enjoying her first sound sleep in ages, Mama had rattled the knob and called out for her deceased husband until Felicity surrendered. She had never locked the door again.

"Are we getting all settled in?" A plump nurse in a pink uniform stood in the doorway, a clipboard in her hands.

"Yes, I think so. I've got her clothes all put away—except her bathrobe. I hung that on the back of the door. Mama likes her afternoon soaps, so she'll probably sit here contentedly for a while."

"Glad to hear it." The nurse entered the room and perused the photos Felicity had placed on Mama's dresser. She picked up one taken of her parents on their wedding day, Mama in a suit and matching hat. "Did I hear a British accent when she spoke earlier?"

"Yes. Mama always called herself a 'late bloomer'—the only forty-year-old war bride in history."

"Your father's very handsome."

"Isn't he? He was a captain when they met. He died when I was twelve, so it's been just the two of us."

Felicity showed the nurse a photo of Queen Elizabeth with the Duke of Edinburgh, Prince Charles, and Princess Anne. "Mama snapped this picture five years ago when they were here for Manitoba's centennial."

"I remember. Is that Lower Fort Garry?"

"Yes. We went to see the royal family, and she managed to get this great shot. She's so proud of it. Seeing them was one of the highlights of her life. She remarked often about how she'd never laid eyes on any of the royals as long as she lived in Great Britain. She had to come all the way to North America to see them." She chuckled. "She was so much better then."

Felicity replaced the picture, and the nurse looked at another. "Is this you with your parents?"

"Yes. Mama loves this picture of the three of us. I was about six here, I think. We were visiting the English gardens at Assiniboine Park. I've taken her back many times. I suppose I should try to get a new photo of us there before she's unable to go any more. A colored one, this time."

"Well, I'm sure she'll be up for an outing at some point. But we don't recommend it too soon. Let her settle in and feel at home here before confusing her with more coming and going. It will be a big adjustment." The nurse laid a hand on Felicity's arm. "For both of you."

Felicity nodded, not trusting her voice. She stayed until Mama dozed off. The sky grew dark with heavy rain clouds, appropriate to her mood. She pulled into the driveway and sat in her car, staring at the old house. The peeling paint offered a sad metaphor for Mama's condition. But while the house could be restored, Mama would only continue to deteriorate until she breathed her last.

With a heavy sigh, she finally dragged herself out of the car and into the house just as the rain began to fall. She flipped on the kitchen light and heard a welcoming meow. Charlie, Mum's fourteen-year-old white Persian, rubbed against her leg.

"Hello, Chuck." Felicity turned on the radio and opened a can of cat food as Captain and Tennille sang about how love would keep them together, whatever.

Love hasn't kept me together with anyone. Life is just a long series of goodbyes.

Determined to lift the gloom, she walked from room to room turning on every lamp. In the living room, the jigsaw puzzle she and Mama had begun two years earlier still sat, unfinished, on a folding table in the corner. She hadn't touched it in months and couldn't remember the last time they'd worked on it together. Maybe now she could finish the puzzle and finally box it up.

She studied the picture on the front of the box, propped up against the wall. The girl gazing down the wishing well looked as though she hadn't a care in the world, surrounded by beautiful flowers on a glorious, sunny summer day. Someone who loved this girl deeply had painted her portrait many years before. Whoever she was, she'd probably be an old lady by now. Like Mama.

Chapter Fifteen

She'd had every intention of returning to tuck Mama into bed for her first night in her new surroundings. But the combination of the rain on the roof and the music from the radio in the next room—not to mention the sheer emotional exhaustion of taking this huge step that could never be reversed—had lulled Felicity to sleep on the sofa. When the clock on the mantel chimed eleven, she jumped to her feet. How could she have let this happen?

She sank back onto the sofa. It was much too late to go now. Visiting hours were long over. Hopefully, Mama had settled down easily enough. No one had phoned, so she would assume the best. But a whole new load of guilt landed on her shoulders.

"I suppose this is my new reality, Chuck," she said as the cat leapt to the sofa like a youngster. "I might have my own life back, but I feel guilty no matter what I do." She stroked the cat, grateful for some life in the house. How long before she'd need to say goodbye to him too? "It's too quiet around here, don't you think?"

The cat curled into his sleep position and ignored her.

"Fine." She turned off the lights and wandered back into the kitchen. An Elton John song was playing, reminding Felicity yet again of her mother's homeland. Mama had never returned, and Felicity had never visited. Never met any of her English relatives, never saw the bombed-out part of London where Mama had worked as a secretary before meeting Felicity's father. Though they'd spoken often of how they'd visit "one day," it never came. Now it never would.

Her stomach rumbling, she opened the fridge to see what might be handy to eat. Bottles of every imaginable sauce and condiment lined the door. Covered margarine and cottage cheese containers holding leftovers that had been there for weeks crowded the shelves. Felicity groaned. It would be easier to clean the fridge out completely, maybe just toss everything without even checking the contents of all these containers. With a sigh, she grabbed a small carton of milk and emptied it over a bowl of Cheerios.

"What I need is a plan," she mumbled around a mouthful of cereal, standing with her back against the kitchen counter. Tomorrow was Sunday. She'd check in on Mama first thing, then attend church alone. After church, she'd clean this kitchen from top to bottom, then return to spend the evening with Mama. On Monday, she'd shop for groceries after school. After that, she'd tackle one room at a time, sorting through the clutter and cleaning as time allowed. Somehow, she needed to bring fresh life into this house, or she'd go crazy.

"And I'll start with that stupid puzzle," she muttered as she switched off the lights and the radio and headed up the stairs to bed. "Maybe I'll give it to Dan Gordon."

Dan, one of the teachers at her school, liked jigsaw puzzles and usually had one set up in his classroom for students to work on when they finished their assignments. At the start of each year, he liked to tell his class a story from his childhood about how his younger brother had driven him nuts by stealing a puzzle piece so he could drop in the final one when everyone else had done all the work. If she remembered his story right, he and his brother each stole and stubbornly hung onto a piece one year until their weary mother put the unfinished puzzle away.

Then he'd motivate the students by offering jawbreakers to the whole class if they completed the puzzle with no stolen pieces. Yes. Maybe she'd give Mama's puzzle to Dan, provided it was all there.

At church on Sunday, Felicity felt strange sitting in the pew without Mama. But for the first time in ages, she began to take note of the people around her. Because Mama's dementia had come so early in life, her friends were still relatively young. Many of them expressed love and encouragement to Felicity, patting her shoulder and telling her she had done the right thing. Asking how they could help.

A large number of young people, including two of her own students, livened up the congregation. She'd been only vaguely aware that the church had a youth pastor, and today he walked onto the platform to welcome everyone.

"Hi, everybody, my name is Reggie Gordon. I think most of you know I'm the youth pastor here."

He had to be related to Dan Gordon at work! They looked so much alike. Was he the little brother who liked to steal puzzle pieces? Maybe she'd get a chance to ask him later.

The man continued. "We've got a special treat today. Our very own wonderful young people will be leading the service. God's been doing a lot of neat things in their hearts, and they want to share some of their music and stories with us."

That explained the drums on stage. Well, this was disappointing. Felicity had come to church for a bit of encouragement to help her through the week—some wise words from the pastor that she could carry with her through the difficult days. Maybe some sense of absolution for having abandoned her mother. What could a bunch of kids offer?

For the next fifteen minutes, she endured what she'd heard the youth refer to as "Jesus Freak" music. She wouldn't have minded if it had been done well, but these kids clearly needed some practice. Maybe she'd find an opportunity to slip out and start on her projects at home. But when the singing ended, a boy she recognized from school—who held a reputation as a trouble-maker—stood to tell his story, arousing Felicity's curiosity.

"Hi, everyone, I'm Kirk. I'm going to read the scriptures today, but first I want to say thank you to the people of this church who pray for us youth. And thanks for hiring Pastor Reggie. He's been a big help to me. A year ago, I was suspended from school and headed down a pretty bad path. I'm sure I wouldn't be back in school now if it weren't for your prayers and for Pastor Reggie. He helped me get right with God, and I'm glad to say, I'm now a leader in this group, and I'll be graduating in June."

A round of applause went up, along with the odd "Praise the Lord" from the congregation. Then Kirk read from Psalm 40 in a new paraphrase called *The Living Bible*. Felicity glanced around the room. How would this "King James only" crowd react? To her surprise, the adults responded with smiles and nods. She turned her attention back to Kirk and listened.

"'I waited patiently for God to help me; then he listened and heard my cry. He lifted me out of the pit of despair, out from the bog and the mire, and set my feet on a hard, firm path, and steadied me as I walked along. He has given me a new song to sing, of praises to our God. Now many will hear of the glorious things he did for me, and stand in awe before the Lord, and put their trust in him.'"

Kirk closed his Bible and returned to his seat while another teen, a girl, rose to the platform. One after the other, kids got up and shared how God was at work in their lives and how they now wanted to make a difference in the world. One girl said she wanted to become a nurse specializing in care for the elderly. It seemed like a unique interest for someone so young until she explained.

"I watched my grandmother become very confused." She flipped her long blonde hair back over her shoulder. "People called her senile. But I knew she was still in there, the same woman I had always loved, the woman who had survived two wars and who had raised seven children. I want to do whatever I can to ensure that people don't suffer the same indignities I saw Grandma go through before she died. I believe this is the work God is calling me to do."

Felicity felt a tear on her cheek and brushed it away. Before she knew it, the morning was over. They closed with one more song, and this time, the music sounded much better to her ears. Pastor Reggie prayed a blessing over the young people, thanking God for them and the various callings on their lives.

She walked home with their stories running through her mind. Maybe those kids had more to offer than she gave them credit for. *God, if they can trust you at this stage of their lives, so can I. Show me your path and help me walk with you.*

It wasn't until she arrived home that she remembered she had wanted to ask Reggie if he was Dan Gordon's brother, the pesky puzzle piece thief.

Chapter Sixteen

Felicity filled the biggest mug she could find with coffee and sat down at the puzzle table. The kitchen cleaning could wait. With CBC radio playing mellow music and Charlie curled up nearby, she was determined to finish the puzzle, then dismantle it and box it up. The removal of Mama's chair had already left a vacant spot on the carpet. Once the puzzle and the folding table were gone, she'd rearrange the room into a less cluttered and more modern-looking space.

As she worked, she thought about the knickknacks she would box up and how she'd make the room her own. Maybe a fresh coat of paint? Perhaps even covering the old worn hardwood with some of that new shag carpeting? She dismissed the idea. Mama wasn't gone yet, after all. Technically, it was still Mama's house. And much of Felicity's time would still be taken up by her mother. It just wouldn't be *here*. Better to leave the more ambitious projects alone for now. Painting wasn't her forte, anyway.

As the picture in front of her neared completion, Felicity could easily imagine the artist who painted it. Probably a middle-aged woman, remembering herself as a young girl. Longing for a return to innocence, for a time when making wishes was still filled with hope. She picked up the lid of the puzzle box but could find only the manufacturer—Merry Times Amusements, Minneapolis. No artist. Strange. It was exquisite work. She flipped the lid over. Stuck to the inside with brittle, yellow tape was a receipt from Salty's Pawn Shop. Felicity had never heard of the place and doubted Mama had ever stepped inside a pawn shop in her life. The hand-written date and the dollar amount were too faded to read. How had this old puzzle come to be in their house? Maybe Dad had brought it home back in the forties, and it had sat on a closet shelf for years. Maybe one of Mama's friends had given it to her more recently, hoping the mental activity would keep her mind active.

With a sigh, Felicity began to suspect she was going to be short a piece. Blue sky constituted the last bit of open space, and she had five puzzle pieces left. One by one, she found where they went. Sure enough, a hole the shape and size of one piece remained. She lifted the box and looked around on the floor beneath the table. Nothing. A quick search of the room revealed only bits of lint and cat hair. In frustration, Felicity opened the door to Mama's bedroom for the first time since Mama left the house.

She couldn't bring herself to step inside. The room was neat and tidy, the dresser-top bare. She'd gone through all Mama's drawers and closet shelves when she'd packed for her move to the nursing home. If a puzzle piece lay hidden in this room, she'd have found it then.

Charlie rubbed against her leg as he ran by, then took a leap onto Mama's bed. His single *meow* seemed to hold a question mark at the end.

"I know, Chuck. I miss her too."

The cat curled up as if to say, "I'll just wait right here for her."

Felicity left the bedroom door wide open as a first step. Maybe she'd eventually make it her own room and save herself a lot of stair-climbing, but that was in the future. She spent another fifteen minutes searching the whole house, knowing one lone puzzle piece couldn't have gone far. Her frustration grew as the time neared to leave.

"I'm setting a timer, Chuck," she said when the cat materialized at her feet again. "I'm giving this stupid puzzle another ten minutes of my life, and then it goes back into the box, finished or not."

She found the old Lux Minute Minder Mama had always used for baking cookies and set it for ten minutes. Then she completed another circuit of the house, upstairs and down. She opened cupboards and drawers, looked under beds and in closets. She even checked the bathroom medicine cabinet.

"It was probably missing before the puzzle ever entered this house," she muttered. "I'm wasting my time."

When the timer dinged, Felicity sighed with relief and marched over to the puzzle table. It took her no time at all to break the puzzle back up into five hundred pieces—make that four hundred ninety-nine—and toss them into the box. She set the lid firmly in place.

"I can't in good conscience give this to anyone at school now, Chuck." She carried it to the kitchen. "Especially Dan Gordon. His students would have no chance of finishing the puzzle and earning jaw breakers."

She could take it with her to Shady Grove. Most of the residents there wouldn't know whether a puzzle was complete or not—if they even lived long enough to finish one. It might not be the most charitable thought, but it was true. She tossed the box into her tote bag along with the bulletin from that morning's church service, a banana for Mama, and a book for herself.

"Be good, Chuck. I'll be back in a couple of hours." She locked the door behind her.

Mama was asleep when she arrived, so Felicity pulled out the puzzle box and went to the nurse's station. A middle-aged nurse with curly hair and a pink uniform looked up from a clipboard and smiled.

"Hi." Felicity held out the box. "I thought the residents might enjoy this puzzle. It's at least forty years old, I think."

"Oh, isn't that pretty?" The nurse nodded toward an open lounge area at the end of the hall. "You can add it to the shelf with the others."

Felicity placed the puzzle on a shelf with half a dozen others, board games, decks of cards, and books. Back in Mama's room, she sat reading until Mama began to stir.

"Hi, Mama."

Mama blinked at her a few times, and Felicity picked up her glasses from the bedside table and helped her put them on. "Did you have a good nap?" Then she repeated the drill the staff had taught her to do every time she came or each time Mama woke up. "I'm Felicity, your daughter. You're at the Shady Grove care home. It's Sunday afternoon."

"I know you're my daughter." Mama huffed. "You don't have to tell me."

"Oh, that's good!" Felicity smiled. "That's really good."

Mama gazed at her a moment. "What's your name again?"

"Felicity." She tried not to sigh. After helping Mama to the bathroom, she pulled out the church bulletin and told her about the morning service with the young people. "That new youth pastor is a go-getter."

Her mother nodded. "That's good."

"Isn't it?" She continued to read the bulletin aloud, as if it would make any difference to Mama whether the church was holding a bake sale or the youth group was flying to the moon. At least it was conversation. Sort of.

When nothing remained to read, Felicity took Mama for a walk down the hallway and back.

"Hey, it's time for *Hymn Sing*." Felicity turned on the little TV and found the CBC program Mama never missed. She used to brag about how the show's music director, Eric Wild, had conducted a revue for the Royal Canadian Navy during the war. Felicity's father had seen the revue in person more than once. Now Eric Wild was right here in Winnipeg, conducting the CBC symphony orchestra for radio and live concerts, as well as this weekly TV program.

As Felicity knew she would, Mama sat captivated by the small choir and soloists, singing along to most of the old hymns. Memory was a funny thing. If only she had a way to record the shows and replay them for Mama throughout the week.

She stayed long enough to see Mama settled in for the night, alleviating her guilt about missing the previous night. Before turning out the light, she picked up Mama's Good News Bible and read to her from Isaiah 46. "Listen to me, descendants of Jacob, all who are left of my people. I have cared for you from the time you were born. I am your God and will take care of you until you are old and your hair is gray. I made you and will care for you; I will give you help and rescue you."

She kissed Mama's forehead and turned off the bedside lamp. Then she had a candid conversation with the nurse who helped put Mama to bed.

"She's doing really well," the nurse said. "Often, new patients are so disoriented, they refuse to sleep at all."

Felicity returned home with a lighter heart. Charlie met her at the door, and she opened a can of cat food for him and a can of chicken noodle soup for herself. After eating, she peered into the overcrowded fridge. Enough time and energy remained in the day to clean out the refrigerator.

"It will feel so good to have this done, Chuck. Tomorrow after school, I'll go straight to the store for groceries and have a nice clean fridge to put them in." She filled a pail with warm water and some baking soda to wipe down the inside of the fridge. "But first—to purge ourselves of all this."

She grabbed a large, black trash bag and began filling it with various containers, contents unknown. Withered apples, moldy carrots—all of it went straight into the bag. She checked the *best before* dates on every condiment and tossed in every expired thing. It felt good. Like progress. New beginnings. When she got to the crisper drawer at the bottom of the fridge, a mesh bag of onions looked salvageable, and she set it aside. She picked through bits of onion skin, gathering them into the bag.

Then her jaw dropped.

"Oh, for cryin' out loud. How did this get here?"

In the bottom of the crisper lay a sky-blue puzzle piece.

She shook her head. How many more things would she find in odd places as she cleaned Mama's house? No wonder they called it senility. She dropped the puzzle piece into her purse.

"I'll take this to the nursing home and slip it into the box with the rest of the puzzle tomorrow, Chuck. Don't let me forget."

Chapter Seventeen

Felicity hauled that puzzle piece around in her purse for three months. She'd see it there when she paid for gas or groceries, when she reached for her lipstick before returning to class after lunch, or at church while digging for a pen to take sermon notes. But never when she was at the nursing home where she could return it to its rightful place.

Mama had been declining rapidly in recent weeks and never spoke anymore. Felicity would sit with her and show her photos of the changes she was making at the house. She was quite proud of the way she'd spruced up the living room and updated the kitchen. Coral paint now covered three walls, while bright orange, yellow, and green wallpaper flowers popped from the fourth. The matching curtains Felicity had sewn and hung over the sink completed her project. The brighter room invited her to enjoy spending time there. Maybe she'd even host a Tupperware party and invite all the female teachers from her school. Best of all, she now slept soundly at night. As a result, things were going much better at school.

She'd told Mama all this and more, such as how Mama's friends at church continued to ask about her and how Felicity always encouraged them to visit. They all said the same thing, "I'll do that," but then never did. To her knowledge, only the pastor ever came. Or he was the only one who took time to sign the guest book she'd left open on the dresser. Mama gave no evidence that she knew or remembered who came and went.

Finally, one Sunday afternoon, Felicity pulled into Shady Grove's parking lot. Before climbing out of the car, she fished the puzzle piece from her bag and clutched it in her hand. She walked straight to the lounge, found the box with the young lady at the wishing well, and placed the piece inside. Apparently, no one had yet opened the box or tried to assemble the puzzle.

With that off her mind, she headed down the hall toward her mother's room. As she rounded the corner, a nurse exited Mama's room and closed the door behind her softly.

"Is she asleep?"

The nurse, a Jamaican immigrant whose warmth had won Felicity over early on, did not return her smile. "Oh, I was just going to try calling you again. There was no answer earlier."

"I was at church. Is Mama all right?"

The nurse lay a hand on Felicity's arm. "I'm so sorry. Your mother has passed."

Surely, she'd heard wrong. "Excuse me?"

The nurse guided her into the nearest chair just outside Mama's door and crouched beside her. "She had a really peaceful night, no reason for us to call you or suspect she was getting close. But when I went into her room not twenty minutes ago, she was gone. I'm so sorry."

Felicity froze. How was that possible? The evening before, when she'd stopped in to visit, she'd been in a hurry, eager to prep the bathroom walls for painting. Had she even noticed how Mama was doing? Had she touched her? Had she said goodbye? Her eyes stung.

"Do you want to see her?"

Felicity looked into the nurse's dark eyes and slowly nodded. Words wouldn't come.

"I know it's a shock, even when you expect it—and you weren't expecting it, not yet—it's hard. I'll go with you. You can take all the time you need."

Felicity stepped into the now-familiar room, the nurse by her side. With the curtains tightly closed, the warm glow of a corner lamp provided just enough light to see the still form on the bed. Mama had become so tiny in recent weeks, it seemed almost as though a child lay there. But as she slowly moved her focus along the soft pink blanket toward Mama's face, it became clear that this was only a shell. Though her wrinkled skin and curly gray hair were the same, her spirit had vanished.

"Did she die in her sleep?"

"I believe so," the nurse said. "Her eyes were closed when I found her. You can touch her if you like."

Felicity moved forward and took hold of Mama's left hand, already cool to the touch. She stroked each finger. The wedding ring that had long been too large to stay in place lay in Felicity's jewelry box at home. Mama had never willingly taken it off, even though she'd been a widow nearly thirty years.

The nurse slid a chair nearer to the bed for Felicity. "Is there someone I can call for you? Pastor Wilson?"

Felicity looked up. "Oh. Yes. That would be good. Thank you."

"I'm sure he'll come as soon as he can. Stay as long as you like. I'll put a placard on the door so no one disturbs you."

The nurse left, and Felicity took a seat. Mama's lifeless face brought to mind events from her childhood, her teen years. With no siblings and with a preference for books over social activities, Felicity had made few friends. Certainly, no one she'd call a best friend. At ten, her parents had insisted a week at summer Bible camp would be good for her. She'd become so homesick, they came and picked her up after the third day, and she never returned. Felicity had even lived at home through her college years, finally renting her own apartment once she started teaching, just minutes away.

When Mama's increasing need for care precipitated Felicity's return home, their relationship had run the gamut of dependence and co-dependence. She'd heard more than one fellow teacher comment about the inordinate amount of time they spent together. Whenever there was a school function after hours or a social event, Felicity was too busy with Mama to join in. Was it excessive? Unhealthy? What did *normal* look like, if not the way they'd done it? She had no clue.

A light tap at the door pulled Felicity out of her reverie. "Come in." She looked up to greet Pastor Wilson.

But the young youth pastor entered the room. "Felicity?"

She nodded. *What was his name? Robbie? Reggie?*

"I'm Reg Gordon. I believe we've met once or twice at church?" He held out one hand as if to shake hers, then thought better of it and brushed it through his longish hair. "Pastor Wilson sent me. He went straight home to bed after church, I'm afraid. Sounds like it might be a flu." He looked around the room. "I'm so sorry about your mother."

"Thank you for coming," Felicity murmured, disappointed. Mama had belonged to the church for forty years. Surely, she deserved someone with more experience. "Will you be doing the funeral?"

"Only if Pastor Wilson isn't up to it. He said to tell you how sorry he is that he couldn't come here today. He had a lot of respect and fondness for your mother." The young pastor pulled up a chair and sat near the foot of the bed. "I imagine you're still in a bit of shock."

"Yes." She'd been so young when her father died, she had no idea where to start with all the practical things that needed to be done.

"You don't have to open this now." The young pastor pulled a large envelope out from under one arm and held it out to Felicity. "But go ahead and take it for later. Your mother pre-arranged her funeral with Robbins' Funeral Services and left this with the church. Pastor Wilson told me where to find it. I'm sure everything in there will make things easier for you. They always do a very professional job."

"Thank you." Felicity looked at the envelope and sighed. "I didn't even know Mama did this. I wonder why she gave it to him rather than to me?"

Reggie paused. "Maybe out of love, to spare you having to think about it sooner than necessary."

"Mmm." Felicity nodded. She could imagine Mama thinking that way.

"I wish I'd had a chance to get to know her. She was British, wasn't she?"

"That's right." Felicity smiled. "A war bride, although she joked about that because she was much older than the others. My father was an officer when they met over there."

"Do you have sisters or brothers?"

"No. It's just me."

"Cousins? Aunts, uncles?

"Mama's family are in England. I don't know any of them. Dad lost his only brother in the war. He still has a sister in Ontario somewhere, I think. We've lost touch."

Reggie Gordon's gaze never left Felicity's face. "That's unfortunate. Family can be such a source of strength and support at times like this."

"Mm," Felicity murmured. "I suppose. You can't really miss what you never had."

They sat quietly awhile, and Felicity almost felt sorry for Reggie Gordon. Surely, he was out of his element. "Do you still have your parents?"

His eyes sparkled when he smiled. "My mother, yes. She raised my brother and me after Dad died in the war. I never knew him."

Felicity nodded. Well, this youth pastor must be older than she thought. Maybe even her own age. "Thank you for all you're doing for our young people. I wish there'd been such a thing as youth pastors when I was a kid."

Now Reggie's face really lit up. "Me too! We didn't have a youth pastor when I was a teen, but I am thrilled to be one now. I can't imagine doing anything else." When he raised his hands to gesture, the glint of a wedding ring caught Felicity's eye.

"You have a family of your own?"

Reggie looked at the ring and grinned. "The ring is a prop. My mother's idea."

"Really?"

He dipped his chin, and his face grew red. "She thought it might be a good idea, at least to start. Teenage girls can get ideas, apparently."

Felicity let out a soft chuckle. "I see. But ... aren't they beginning to wonder where Mrs. Gordon is?"

"Exactly. I think it's time to leave the ring at home. I never was comfortable with the deception."

"Not one of your mom's better ideas?"

"She meant well." Reggie removed the ring and tucked into the front pocket of his shirt. "Got this at a pawn shop for five dollars." He patted the pocket gently. "No wife or kids for me yet. My brother's got two girls, six and four, for Mum to spoil. He's a teacher like you, so we both work with kids."

"I think I might work with your brother." Felicity cocked her head. "Dan?"

"That's right. I still call him Danny." Reggie stopped and grimaced. "Sorry. I'm not here to talk about me. What can I do for *you*?"

Felicity took a deep breath and slowly moved her head from side to side. "I don't even know." They both looked at the still form on the bed again. "I wish I'd been here when she died. I left in such a hurry last night, I—I had no idea. I was so focused on my own stuff, my own—" Her voice cracked. "My own life. What if she needed me in those final moments?" She rose and laid a hand on her mother's soft curls.

"Pastor Wilson told me you've been an incredibly dedicated daughter. You've got no reason to feel guilty. No one could have known last night was her last."

His kind words released Felicity's tears. "Thank you for saying that. It helps."

"She looks very peaceful."

Felicity nodded. "She loved the Lord more than anything."

Reggie moved to stand beside her, placing one hand on her shoulder and the other on Mama's arm. Then he began to pray with far more fervency than Felicity would have ever expected. "God, thank you for taking this child of yours home in such a peaceful manner. Thank you that she had a wonderful and devoted daughter to care for her. I ask that your comforting arms would enfold Felicity now. Be near her as she grieves this loss. Thank you that your word says you comfort the orphans, that you are a father to the fatherless. May your people rally around her. May she experience peace, and may she know how dearly loved she is by you. In Jesus' name, amen."

Felicity murmured *amen* and wiped tears from her cheeks.

"If you like, I can tell the staff you're ready for them to call the funeral home."

Though she merely nodded, peace flooded Felicity's heart. She may have lost Mama, but that didn't mean she was all alone.

Chapter Eighteen

Wishing Well, Manitoba. June 1975.

*R*ay Matthews jiggled one knee as he waited in the pew on the bride's side. He'd been inside this church only five times since Mum's funeral—once for each of his nieces' and nephews' weddings. At twenty-six, Pearl was the last of the bunch to take this step, and Ray hoped it would be the last time he'd have to come here. After all, he didn't welcome God into his house, so why on earth would God welcome Ray into *his*? The sooner the ceremony was over, the sooner he could get out.

As he'd done at the other weddings, Ray would shuffle over to the community hall with the other guests, enjoy a meal, and listen to the toasts. Then he'd disappear before they cleared the floor for dancing. With any luck, he'd slip away without having to speak to Caroline. He'd stop to check on Sarah's wishing well, make a note of any work it might need, pull weeds from around its base. Then, before heading home to do his evening chores, he'd stop at the cemetery to tell Sarah all about Pearl's wedding. She was, after all, marrying one of the Martindale boys. Sarah's nephew, born long after her passing.

Our families will finally be joined, Sarah. Isn't that swell?

After their falling out in the late fifties, Caroline had continued to invite Ray to Christmas dinners, birthday parties, and graduations. He usually showed up, but he remained focused on the youngsters. As the kids grew up and moved out one by one, the invitations had slowed and finally stopped. Ray couldn't recall the last time he'd been inside his sister's home, and it was even longer since she'd set foot in his. When they did speak, it was polite enough. But it was never comfortable.

The organ music began, and the congregation rose. Ray's heart pounded when Pearl appeared on her father's arm. She was radiant. For an instant, Ray wanted to capture this moment forever on canvas. But just as quickly, he brushed the thought away. Instamatic cameras clicked all around him, doing the job far more efficiently and accurately. At sixty-two, Ray's hands were too shaky to paint even if he wanted to.

The beautiful bride approached the front, reminding Ray so much of Caroline in her youth. She smiled at the guests, her loving gaze returning to her waiting groom every few seconds. When she walked past Ray, their eyes connected for just a moment, and he smiled back.

What must it be like?

Ray took his seat with the others when the pastor invited them to sit, but he heard little of the scriptures or the advice the man offered the couple. His thoughts were fixed on what had never been his. Never would be his. Was Caroline right? Could he have found someone to share his life if he'd let go of Sarah? Should he have tried harder?

He shook the thought off. It was impossible. Not only could he not give up Sarah's hold on him, but he couldn't reconcile his convictions. No serious Christian woman would ever be interested in a man who wanted nothing more to do with God. Yet nothing less than a God-fearing woman would ever capture Ray's affection.

Even Ray could see the ridiculous double standard.

You're just an old fool, Ray Matthews. He'd thought it often enough. He knew he was Wishing Well's laughingstock. He was the community's surly old bachelor living like a hermit in the rotting farmhouse, devoting every resource he had to the memory of a long-lost love. He was the one kids got teased about. He'd heard the taunts when he walked past the school playground and the stage-whispered gossip around town. *Look out, or you'll end up like ol' Ray Matthews. ... If she doesn't hurry and find herself a man, she'll end up with ol' Ray Matthews.* Did they all assume Ray was deaf? Even the Martindale family thought he was off his rocker.

They're probably right. But it's too late for me now.

That last time he'd been at one of his sister's Christmas gatherings, Pearl's siblings had teased her that she'd remain a spinster. Told her she better make a lot of money and leave it all to her nieces and nephews, who now numbered eleven—if Ray wasn't forgetting anyone. And if he wasn't mistaken, one of them looked as though she might be expecting another.

Mum and Dad would be so proud of all these offspring. *And not a one to carry on the Matthews name.* Ray could almost hear Dad's disappointment. His dreams for Ray had been bigger than his own—to be a famous artist, a loving husband and father, and most of all, a devoted Christian.

Ray had failed on every point.

He turned his focus to the groom, a man of thirty named Brian Martindale. Although some branch of the Martindales still ran the family farm here at Wishing Well, Pearl had met Brian in Winnipeg where they both worked in a law office. That was all Ray knew about him, but now that he saw him, the family resemblance was obvious. As was the young man's love for Pearl. His devotion sparkled in his eyes as he smiled at her, taking in her beauty.

Just think, Sarah. My niece and your nephew, carrying on the Martindale name. If they have children, I might get a glimpse of what ours would have looked like.

Half a dozen huge bouquets of lilacs graced the space across the front, filling the room with their sweet fragrance. The pastor was reading a Bible passage from one of those modern paraphrases, and Ray tried to tune it out by focusing on the flowers.

"'Love is very patient and kind, never jealous or envious, never boastful or proud...'"

Two large, electric fans whirred, oscillating back and forth in a hypnotic rhythm against the heat of the June day.

"'...never haughty or selfish or rude. Love does not demand its own way. It is not irritable or touchy.'"

Three bridesmaids, staggered in height, stood like wildflowers in matching, multi-colored dresses that hung to their ankles. Each held a bouquet of brilliant peonies and wore baby's breath in her hair.

"'It does not hold grudges and will hardly even notice when others do it wrong. It is never glad about injustice, but rejoices whenever truth wins out.'"

The little ring-bearer—one of Caroline's grandsons—shuffled his feet in his polished black shoes and tugged at the collar of his miniature tuxedo. He waved his satin pillow around like an airplane until one of the groomsmen bent down to whisper in his ear and to hold the pillow still. As soon as the man straightened, the airplane motions began again. Ray chuckled. Hopefully, the rings were tied on tight.

"'If you love someone, you will be loyal to him no matter what the cost...'"

That's right, Sarah. Loyal no matter what the cost. The flames on the tall, white candles flickered every time the fans turned toward them, but they did not blow out. Ray counted them to distract himself—thirty. Fifteen on each of two wooden candelabras that had probably been used for every wedding held in this church since his father first fashioned them forty years ago. Dad would be proud to know they were still being used to add a glow to these special occasions.

"'You will always believe in him, always expect the best of him, and always stand your ground in defending him.'"

In the pews, middle-aged women in pastel dresses fanned themselves with the wedding program. Ray looked down at his, only to see the words of the same passage the pastor was reading. He turned his attention to the stained-glass windows.

"'All the special gifts and powers from God will someday come to an end, but love goes on forever.'"

Hear that, Sarah? Love goes on forever. Everybody said so, even the good book. Why couldn't anyone see that? Why was Ray's forever-love seen as sad and pathetic?

The bride and groom exchanged vows and rings, much to the obvious relief of the little boy who sat down beside his parents in the second row. While the couple signed the papers, one of the bridesmaids sang "We've Only Just Begun" while another accompanied her on the piano. Ray had heard the Carpenters sing it on the radio in his kitchen while he waited for the news, and it always struck a sad chord in his heart.

The organ took up the wedding march, and the congregation rose. The bridal party charged to the back of the church, faces aglow. Pearl and her new husband were all smiles. Ray was certain he saw Sarah's eyes and dimple on the groom's face.

Members of the two immediate families followed. Ray caught a glimpse of Caroline wiping tears from her cheeks. She slipped her arm through her husband's and smiled up at him. His sister had found a good mate and made a great life for herself. Ray was glad. When her eyes met his for the briefest of moments, he didn't look away. Instead, he allowed himself to feel the longing for family, for connection.

Enough time has passed. The thought seemed so foreign, Ray glanced up at one of the stained-glass windows, wondering where it had come from. *Caroline won't bother you about letting go of Sarah anymore. She'll leave you be. There's no need to lose your sister too.*

He looked back at her just as she glanced over her shoulder at him. The warmth of her smile unlocked something so definitively, Ray could have sworn he heard a soft *click* somewhere in the vicinity of his heart.

That evening, Ray did not leave the wedding dance early as he'd planned. In fact, when Pearl pulled him to his feet with a "come dance with the bride, Uncle Ray," he awkwardly allowed her to lead him once around the room. Amazingly, dark had fallen by the time he left, and he did not stop at the wishing well or the cemetery.

I'll do it tomorrow. Right after I stop by and visit my sister.

Part 4: 1999

Dean

Chapter Nineteen

Winnipeg

Dean Jacobs tightened his fingers around his mobile phone. He could throttle his sister. Dad had been gone a month. A *month!* And Samantha had done absolutely nothing about the state of Dad's horrible apartment. Had she even stepped foot inside this place? Now the landlord was breathing down their necks, and Dean couldn't blame him. He'd paid the man for another month just to settle him down.

He stood in the middle of Dad's hoarded piles, barely able to turn around while he talked to Samantha.

"Have you been over here at all, Sam? I couldn't even find Dad's phone to call you." Dean turned another three-sixty, running one hand through his hair. Exhausted from his early morning flight, he had little patience for this.

He could picture Sam's face as she let out a growl. "First of all, I was over there every single day while he was still alive. I've purged that apartment more times than I can count. Where were *you* all that time?"

"Not fair. You live here, I don't."

"—and secondly, even if you did find Dad's phone, you'd find it out of service. I took care of that."

"Oh. Well, I guess that makes—"

"And thirdly...you obviously have a cell phone, so what's the big deal?"

"It's supposed to be for work."

"Which is all you ever think about. Mister Big-Shot, taking off for China almost before the funeral was even over—"

Dean huffed. "I told you. I had already postponed the trip a whole week to deal with funeral arrangements. It couldn't wait any longer! I figured the least you could do was look after these final details—"

"Details? You call that apartment a *detail*? It's going to take six truckloads to haul away all that junk." Sam's voice broke. "I can't face it alone."

Dean closed his eyes and let out a sigh. Sam was right. No one should have to tackle this alone. The compounded guilt of the last ten years settled on his shoulders again, its familiar weight pressing him down until he was convinced his feet sank beneath the filthy carpet. Trapped. Like Dad had been.

"Sam, I'm sorry. I should have come sooner, I should have—" He sighed again. "Look, we can shoulda, coulda, woulda for the rest of our lives, and it's not going to take care of this. I've paid the rent for another month. I've got a week before I have to be back in Toronto. Can we work on this together?"

A long pause. Had his phone died? "Sis? You there?"

"You've forgotten, haven't you?"

Dean's brain scrambled for an answer, but his silence would certainly confirm that he had, indeed, forgotten whatever she was referring to.

"Michael's grad?" Samantha over-enunciated her words as though speaking to a deaf old man.

Dean looked up at the ceiling and closed his eyes. How could he have forgotten his nephew's high school graduation? This whole trip was supposed to kill two birds with one stone.

"Oh. Right. Um—I only forgot momentarily. Jet lag." What day of the week was it? "That's...tonight, right?"

"Yes. And you'd better be there."

"I will, I will." Dean pulled his little black Daytimer out of his pocket, and it fell open to today's date. *Michael's grad, 6:30 p.m., Sisler High* had been penned in his own tiny scrawl. "That's not 'til tonight, though, right? Could we get started on this in the meantime?"

"Dean! Are you kidding me? I've got a million things to do. I should be on my way to the school right now to help with decorating, then I have a hair appointment at two, and—"

"Of course. Sorry. How does tomorrow look for you?"

Sam sighed yet again. "I have a house full of in-laws. We haven't spent any time with Jack's parents yet, and this is the first time we've seen his brother for a year—"

"Right. Sorry." Something tightened in Dean's chest. He was more of an outsider than ever.

"You have no idea what it's like to have a family."

Ouch.

Dean said nothing, and when Samantha spoke again, her voice had softened.

"I'm sorry. I just—um, Jack's family should be cleared out by Sunday night. I can help on Monday. Do you need a place to stay? You're not sleeping at Dad's, are you?"

"No...no, I'm fine." No way would he sleep here. He'd already checked into the Fairmont and left his bags there. "I know you have a full house. I'll get started over here. We're going to need a truck."

"We can use Jack's. I'll trade vehicles with him on Monday morning."

"And boxes. And cleaning supplies. Lots of them."

"Already thought of both." Samantha cleared her throat. "I need to go. I'll save you a seat at the ceremony tonight, and you're welcome to come over afterward. Michael will be out with his friends, but the rest of us are hanging out here. Jack's built a firepit in the backyard."

"Sounds good." Dean would most likely return to his hotel room after the ceremony. It would be easier than watching someone else's family together, enjoying each other's company. If he was going to feel lonely anyway, it was always less painful to do it alone.

And easier to down half a bottle of vodka.

He said goodbye to his sister and surveyed the apartment one more time. "Okay. One room at a time." He opened the box of large trash bags he'd stopped to buy on his way over and shook one of them wide open with a satisfying snap. *Where to start?*

"Make that one corner at a time."

He moved to the bathroom first. It was the smallest room, and he figured there'd be nothing in it worth keeping. But the stacks of magazines and newspapers jammed in nearly every square inch of floor as well as the bathtub filled six bags all by themselves. *Did you not even bathe, Dad?* Dean shook his head in disgust.

He opened the medicine cabinet and, without even look-ing, scooped every jar and bottle into a trash bag. Numerous half-empty shampoo and lotion containers went in next. Dean dumped a laundry basket overflowing with dirty clothes straight into the bag, then used the basket to collect unopened bars of soap and toilet tissue. At least, those could be donated some-where. A three-year-old calendar and some cheaply framed pic-tures of flowers hung on the walls. He threw those in the bag too. Lastly, he rolled up the shower curtain and scatter rugs, stuffed them all into a bag, and tied it tightly shut.

"I know you're probably howling in protest if you can see me now, Dad," he muttered. "But I can't hear you, so I'm doing this. And I'm making good time."

Dean carried the laundry basket of usable items to his rental car and placed it in the trunk. It was well past noon. No wonder his stomach rumbled. From the deli next door, he grabbed a submarine sandwich and a cup of coffee and returned to the apartment, determined to make another big dent in the mountain.

But the bathroom had been a breeze by comparison to the rest. Dean cleared an armchair loaded down with books so he could sit to eat his sandwich. He surveyed the room while he ate, trying hard not to let it depress him. No wonder Samantha couldn't face this alone.

His gaze fell on the one area that had remained unchanged since Mom's passing—the top shelf of a bookcase just below the window. Although thick with dust, the shelf had always displayed family photos, and they all sat there still, framed in varying sizes and styles. Arranged in chronological order, the row of photos might be the only organized thing in the whole apartment. The oldest was Mom and Dad's wedding photo from 1958, the year before Dean was born. Next was his baby picture, then Samantha's. School pictures followed, and a snapshot of the four of them on a rare family vacation to the World's Fair in Montreal in 1967, Canada's centennial year. Dean retained sharp memories of riding an elevated mini-train over "The Dome of America," built in the middle of the St. Lawrence River. Lumberjacks climbing hundred-foot-high poles had impressed his eight-year-old brain as the epitome of manhood.

Next came high school graduation photos—first his in 1977, then Samantha's a year later. Hard to believe she was now the mother of a graduate. Dean shook away the realization that his Anna would've been graduating soon, too...if she had lived.

The next picture on the shelf was his and Marianne's wedding photo. Why had his parents kept it there even after the divorce? Mom had remained in touch with Marianne for a few years, until she remarried. It seemed cruel to keep the wedding picture on display. He moved on, glancing at Sam and Jack's wedding picture, which was followed by more group photos of Sam's family and school pictures of her kids, Michael and Erica.

No more photos of Dean.

Sipping his coffee, he studied his own wedding picture again. He'd been just twenty, Marianne only nineteen. Much too young to know what they wanted in life. Too immature to know that a baby would not heal the hurts they'd inflicted on each other. And definitely too unequipped to prevent the loss of that baby from tearing them apart completely.

In the least-cluttered corner of the living room, a half-finished jigsaw puzzle sat on Dad's folding table as it always had. Dean stared at it, muffling a chuckle at the irony. The box showed a beautiful young woman gazing down a wishing well. He hadn't seen one of those old-fashioned puzzles made from wood in years. How valuable might it be now? Maybe there was something in this apartment worth salvaging, after all—if the puzzle had all its pieces. But since it was nowhere near finished, there was no way to tell.

Therein lay the irony. The puzzle so accurately represented his father's life. Unfinished. Broken. Bits and pieces of beautiful, unrealized potential. Just like Dean's.

With a sigh, he wadded up his empty cup and sandwich wrapper. To make it through the graduation ceremony later, he needed a nap. And a shower. Time to head back to the hotel. Glancing around for somewhere to leave his trash, he finally tossed it on the floor. What difference did it make? He could deal with all this rubbish tomorrow.

At the last minute before leaving his father's apartment, something compelled him to gather up the unfinished jigsaw puzzle and scoop all the pieces into their box. He stuffed the box into a plastic shopping bag and carried it out with him.

Chapter Twenty

The moment Dean stepped into his old high school, memories flooded him. How was it possible for the place to still smell of mimeograph ink in 1999? Or maybe he smelled sweeping compound or floor wax ... or sweaty bodies. Probably a mingling of all of it. Whatever it was, the fragrance hadn't changed in the twenty-two years since Dean walked out the door for the last time.

Plenty of other things had, though. Through a classroom window, rows of computers sat where he'd once pecked his way through typing class. The lineup of class photos featuring each year's graduates extended far beyond where it once had. Dean resisted the urge to find his own class picture. Marianne's would be right beside it.

In the auditorium-gymnasium, Dean scanned the room until he saw Sam waving him over to the rows reserved for family. He greeted her with a hug and shook his brother-in-law's hand. Beyond Jack sat his extended family, whom Dean acknowledged with a nod and a smile before taking his seat beside Samantha.

"Congratulations. You're on time." She didn't even pretend to be joking.

Dean chose to ignore the barb. "Where's Erica?"

"She's in the band." Sam pointed to the front corner of the room where the band waited to begin. He studied their faces but couldn't spot his niece. Should he admit to Sam that he didn't know which instrument Erica played? He didn't need to.

"Flute section," Sam said in a flat tone.

Dean spotted Erica, who had already spotted him. He smiled and waved back. She'd changed in the short time since Dad's funeral. At fifteen, she'd cut her brown hair short and bleached it blonde. He wouldn't have recognized her if she wasn't waving and smiling at him. At least his niece held nothing against him.

Sam smiled and waved too. "Michael gets to make a speech."

"Really? Valedictorian?"

"No. The class is making a presentation to one of their favorite teachers. She's retiring. They picked Michael to do the honors."

"That's a little unusual, isn't it?"

Sam shrugged. "Maybe, but the grads requested it. They just love Mrs. Gordon."

"Mrs. Gordon?" Dean couldn't believe it. "*The* Mrs. Gordon? She's still here?"

Sam nodded. "Yep. But not for long."

"*I* had Mrs. Gordon. I was here when she *became* Mrs. Gordon. Before that, she was … Miss …" He scanned his memory, but his sister beat him to it.

"Miss Cooper. Yes, I know. Felicity Cooper. I had her too. She married a youth pastor. Reg Gordon? He's just as popular with the kids as she is."

"Wow. Is that why they picked Michael? Second-generation student?"

"I don't know. Maybe. That, and the fact that he's a bit of a comedian." Samantha rolled her eyes.

Dean chuckled. This came as no surprise, but he knew Samantha was proud of her son.

The crowd settled down when the row of dignitaries on stage stood and focused on the back of the gym. The band conductor raised his baton, and the familiar strains of "Pomp and Circumstance" began. Dean swallowed back the lump that never failed to form when he heard it. The crowd stood to watch the procession of graduates. He blinked hard and studied the Spartan logo on the gym wall so he wouldn't have to look at the grads in their caps and gowns.

But Sam wouldn't let him disengage. She tugged on his sleeve and pointed. "There he is!"

Sure enough, Michael had entered the room near the front of the line, tall and handsome in his cap and gown. He made his way down the aisle, grinning all the way. Once all the grads reached their places, the music resolved, and a man Dean could only assume was the principal spoke from the podium. "Please remain standing for 'O Canada.'"

The band played the introduction, and Dean hummed along to the anthem, his eyes on Erica and her flute until the final "on guard for thee." A general shuffle followed as the principal invited everyone to be seated.

Dean relaxed as much as he could on the metal folding chair and allowed his mind to wander throughout the speeches, awards, and presentations of diplomas. When Michael crossed the stage to receive his, he stopped briefly to perform a "Carlton dance," and his classmates cheered. Dean laughed, and then laughed harder at the sight of Samantha's red face. Michael's teachers were probably relieved to see him finishing.

When all the grads had received their diplomas and returned to their seats, an unexpected hush fell over the room. The principal spoke into the microphone again.

"You're probably all expecting to see a hundred and fifty mortarboards tossed into the air right about now, but at the request of the graduates, we have a little surprise first. I'd like to invite Michael Beaudrie to the platform."

Michael was already at the top of the steps, and when he reached the podium, the principal returned to his seat just a few feet behind it. Dean scanned the row of teachers on the platform, trying to figure out if one of them was Felicity Gordon. There were only two women. One was black and the other much too young to be her.

Michael seemed right at home at the microphone. "Thanks, Mr. Robinson." He unfolded a piece of paper and laid it in front of him, then scanned the crowd and smiled. "Before we transmogrify into alumni,"—he began, and the crowd immediately chuckled—"my classmates and I wish to honor someone who has meant the world to us and more than thirty classes before us. Mrs. Felicity Gordon is retiring."

A low murmur trickled through the crowd.

"We, the Class of 1999, feel so fortunate and blessed to have had Mrs. Gordon in our lives these past four years. We like to think we were her favorite class. In fact, I'm pretty sure I was her favorite student." Again, the crowd laughed. "But I also know that's because she had a way of making every student feel that way. I remember the day I walked in late to my very first English class in Grade Nine. She said nothing while I casually took a seat, but at the end of the class, she called me to her desk. She asked my name, and she asked what had happened to make me late.

"The truth was, on the very day that I most wanted to be cool and accepted, I had gotten lost in this place. Turns out, I wasn't even supposed to be in her classroom right then. I had just sat through a Grade Ten class!"

The audience roared and stretched their necks to spot Mrs. Gordon.

Like an experienced comedian, Michael paused until the laughter began to fade. "She had suspected it all along but said nothing. Though I'd never have admitted I got lost to anyone, something about Mrs. Gordon's soft tone and the kindness in her eyes made me feel safe. When I told her the truth, she made sure I knew how to read the map in the front of my binder and how to get to my next class. Then she went with me to see the teacher whose class I had just missed and explained. I felt no condemnation, and I was never late again. Well, not to her class, anyway." Michael's tassel fell across his nose when he moved his head, and he brushed it aside.

"When I ended up in her classroom later that week—in the right class, this time—she asked us to write a paragraph about what we hoped to learn that year. Mine said I just hoped to pass, that I was no good at English, that I'd been told by previous teachers I'd never graduate and should quit dragging other kids down by joking around in class. When I got the paper back, Mrs. Gordon had written a note on the bottom. I still have it."

Michael unfolded a sheet of three-hole punched, lined notebook paper and began to read.

"'Not only will you graduate, Michael, you will do so with honors. I've only just met you, and I can already tell, you have a keen mind, a great sense of humor, and a good heart. Those things will take you far. You can do this! I believe in you.'"

Michael's voice cracked a bit on the last sentence, and he paused. "I guess she was right because here I am in this goofy-lookin' gown with a crazy tassel hangin' in my face."

The crowd laughed, and one of Michael's classmates let out a hoot.

"Mrs. Gordon's investment in her pupils is legendary. She not only got involved in our extracurricular projects, she dragged her husband along. Mr. and Mrs. Gordon joined us on bus rides to basketball games, built sets for the school play, and brought pizza to band rehearsals. They opened their home and refrigerator for so many study sessions, I sometimes wonder how they had any food left for themselves! We always felt welcome.

"And since ours is your last graduating class, Mrs. Gordon, we also benefited from your years of experience. Thanks for not 'checking out' this past year, once you knew you were nearly at the finish line. Thanks for continuing to give your all, right up to the final exams some of us were struggling to write just three days ago. Thank you for taking a genuine interest in our lives, for putting our needs ahead of your own, and for demonstrating the kind of integrity we can model our lives after." He paused to glance around the room.

"This school will miss you. *We'll* miss you. But you deserve a rest, and I'm confident your retirement will be as bright and as meaningful as the way you've lived your whole life. We wish you all the best.

"Mrs. Gordon, will you please come up here so we can present you with a token of our appreciation?"

The crowd rose to its feet and broke into applause. Mrs. Gordon, who must be approaching sixty, stood from her seat somewhere in the middle of the room. She reached back and took her husband's hand and pulled him up beside her. Together, they walked up and stood beside Michael on the platform. One of his female classmates had joined him, carrying a huge bouquet of flowers which she presented to the teacher. Michael pulled a wrapped gift out from under the podium and gave it to her. Finally, the applause faded, and Felicity Gordon spoke into the microphone.

"Thank you, Michael and Rachel. Thank you to the whole class, and thank you to all the classes who have gone before you. You've brought more joy and meaning to my life than you can ever imagine. I've brought Reggie up here with me because he's been my role model in all this. He taught me what it means to invest one's life in youth, in the future of our community, our country, and our world. We've been a team from the beginning, and our work won't stop just because we're retired. In fact, we're looking forward to having more time to help out wherever we can. So don't think you can be rid of me that easily. Thanks again, and God bless every one of you."

Dean swallowed a hard lump as the crowd applauded until long after the Gordons had returned to their seats. How must it feel to be appreciated for building into others that way? He'd never know.

Chapter Twenty-One

The graduates had thrown their caps in the air and formed a line to shake hands and receive congratulations. Not wanting to greet a bunch of kids he didn't know, Dean waited for the line to thin. Then he made a beeline for Michael, plastic bag in hand. He held it out as he spoke and pumped Michael's hand.

"This is the puzzle your grandpa was working on when he passed, Michael. I thought you might like to have it." The story sounded lame even to himself. Michael and Dad hadn't been close, and Dean had no idea whether the boy enjoyed puzzles or not. Probably not. What class clown would ever sit still long enough to work on a puzzle?

"Thanks, Uncle Dean." Michael had returned Dean's handshake, confusion on his face.

"It's an antique," Dean explained. "Might be really valuable one day."

"Cool."

Michael had clearly been taught well and was merely being polite. He accepted the unimpressive gift, and Dean stepped out of the line. Why was he such a screw-up? It would have been better to come empty-handed than to bring such a poorly thought-out gift.

He made his way to a different corner of the room where a crowd was gathering around Felicity and Reg Gordon. He wanted to thank them for their involvement with the kids but also for the encouragement Mrs. Gordon had been to him back in the day. Would she know him? It would probably be just as well if she didn't, because she might recall that he had married Marianne. And she would surely remember Marianne—everyone did. She was beautiful, smart, talented, and the kindest person anyone had ever met. Dean had somehow won Marianne over and then hurt her so badly, she'd been wise to leave. Things would have only gotten worse if she'd stayed. And they had gotten worse, for Dean. He had no desire to talk about his failures now. Still, the pull to connect with the popular Mrs. Gordon felt strong enough to warrant the risk.

He stood apart from the group while current and former students hugged her, and she took time to speak with each one. When someone touched his arm, he turned to see Samantha, her arms laden with Michael's mortarboard, diploma, and gifts.

"We're headed off now, Dean. Will you be joining us at the house?"

Dean hesitated.

"You do remember where we live, right?"

"Funny." His stomach churned at the idea of joining the celebration with Sam's family but grappled for a legitimate excuse to say no. "Sure, I'll be there. Just want to say hello to Mrs. Gordon first."

"Okay." Samantha leaned in. "Marianne came. Did you see her?"

Marianne? Dean hadn't, but he looked around now, scanning the remaining crowd.

"She's gone." Samantha adjusted the load in her arms. "She gave me a card for Michael and slipped out."

"Did she see me?" *What a juvenile thing to say.* But it was too late to retract the words.

"She did."

He stared at his sister but couldn't bring himself to ask.

"You're wondering if she asked about you." Sam raised one eyebrow.

Dean looked at his feet, wanting to deny it but dying to know the answer.

"She didn't. But I told her you were in A.A. and doing much better. Holding down a good job. Going to church."

"Thanks," Dean mumbled. Sam didn't know he'd fallen off the wagon for the umpteenth time and hadn't been to an A.A. meeting in six months or more. Church, even longer.

"Anyway, I'll see you shortly at the house." Sam walked away.

Dean turned again toward the crowd surrounding Mrs. Gordon. If anything, it had grown even larger. He shuffled from one foot to the other and finally changed his mind. She probably wouldn't remember him, anyway. Maybe he'd send her a note later. But even as he thought it, he knew he never would.

He turned in the direction of the door but had only taken a couple of steps when he heard his name.

"Dean? Dean Jacobs, is that you?"

He turned. Mrs. Gordon smiled at him. Walking right through her passel of well-wishers who parted to clear a path, she approached him with the same warmth he'd loved about her back in high school.

"As I live and breathe. It *is* you!" She reached out both hands to take Dean's. "But of course! You're Michael's uncle, aren't you? How could I have forgotten?"

Dean took the woman's soft hands in his. She was still slim, though not as tall as he remembered. Instead of shoulder-length, light-brown hair, she now wore it short and gray. Glasses enhanced fine lines around her eyes, but the sparkle remained.

"Can't expect you to remember all the family connections." He could barely remember them himself. "I'm impressed that you remember me at all."

"Of course, I do. How are you, Dean?"

"I'm well, thanks. I live in Toronto now."

"Michael must be so glad you came all this way." The woman kept holding Dean's hands. "I'm sorry about your father."

Wow, she really did keep tabs on her students. Michael had to miss a basketball game to attend his grandfather's funeral, and Dean vaguely recalled some arguments in his sister's household over that.

Dean nodded. "Thanks. Well, I just wanted to tell you thanks for everything you've done for my nephew and for all the students over the years... me included. You were my favorite teacher. You were everybody's favorite, I think."

Mrs. Gordon laughed. "Oh, not everybody's." Then her smile faded, and she leaned in closer. "I was so sorry that things didn't work out between you and Marianne."

So she knew. Did the whole world know what a jerk he'd been?

"Yeah. Thanks. Well, there are still a lot of folks wanting to talk to you." He pulled his hand away. "I don't want to monopolize your time. But again—thanks for everything, and I wish you all the best in retirement. I'd have brought a card if I'd known."

That was lie too. How would he have ever gotten his act together enough to find a retirement card when he hadn't even bought a graduation card for Michael?

"Don't be silly." Mrs. Gordon shook her head. "I don't need a card. Seeing you is reward enough. I'm so glad you came over to say hello. God bless you, Dean."

"Thanks. Uh—same to you." Dean turned and headed toward the door again. But as he passed by the front row of seats, something caught his eye. The puzzle he'd given Michael lay on one of the folding chairs like a lonely old woman after everyone else had left the party. The bag he'd put it in was nowhere in sight, but Dean had a vague image of his sister stuffing cards and gifts into a similar bag while she spoke with him earlier. He looked around. Samantha, Michael, and the whole family were gone.

Should he just leave the puzzle there? May as well. Maybe the school could use it, or maybe—whatever. It didn't matter. Dean kept walking. When he reached the doors, he took another look over his shoulder toward the front of the room where Mrs. Gordon was still smiling and hugging her devotees. Her husband remained at her side, shaking hands and speaking to people with no sign of impatience or fatigue. The contrast between their lives and Dad's empty, unfinished one—and Dean's own—was stark.

Oh God. I need your help.

Where had that thought come from? Probably from Mrs. Gordon's "God bless you." Without any idea why, Dean strode back to the front row of chairs, picked up the puzzle box, and carried it out with him. He tossed it on the front seat of his car and pulled out of the parking lot. What he wanted more than anything was to find a bottle and return to his hotel room. There'd be no alcohol at Sam's house, and even if there was, he'd be expected to abstain.

"Okay, God. Here's the deal," he said out loud. "If the light on Sophia Street is red when I get there, I'll hang a right and go to Jack and Samantha's house. But if it's green—or even yellow—I'm sailing right on through." Back to his hotel. The hotel with the bar on the main floor.

The odds lay in his favor. Sophia Street was far less traveled than the major street he now drove on. That light was almost never red. He could nearly taste the whiskey already. Only four blocks to go, and he'd be through the intersection and on to his desired destination. He could see the red light already.

Perfect. By the time I get there, it'll be green.

But the light wasn't green. In fact, traffic backed up all the way to Salter, and nobody was moving. What was going on?

Slowly, in fits and starts, Dean inched ahead one more block. He pressed the button to roll his window down and called out to the people in the convertible to his left.

"Any idea what's going on?"

The passenger stretched her neck out of the car. "Light must be stuck. I see a traffic cop up ahead."

Dean muttered as he rolled his window back up. "Very funny. The deal's not over yet. I'm not technically at the light. It could turn green by the time I get there."

Mrs. Gordon's final "God bless you" still rang in his ears.

When he reached the light, he rolled his window down again.

The traffic cop approached him. "It's red both ways. Treat it as a four-way stop."

With a sigh, Dean turned on his blinker. When it was his turn to go, he cranked the steering wheel a hard right, onto Sophia Street.

Chapter Twenty-Two

*D*idn't really think you'd show." Dean's brother-in-law, still in his suit and tie, greeted him at the door with a handshake. "I just gotta say."

You don't actually gotta say. Dean kept the thought to himself.

"C'mon in." Jack Beaudrie waved one arm toward the living room behind him while he closed the door. "You remember my parents, my brother Clint...his wife Audrey."

Around the open space, people sat on sofas or gathered around the island in the middle of the kitchen. He nodded in recognition, although some of them he'd only met once or twice. When he'd served as an usher at Jack and Samantha's wedding twenty years before, a nervous young Clint filled the role of best man. Now he relaxed with an iced tea, watching his two young daughters chase each other around the room with black and gold graduation balloons.

"Hi, Uncle Dean. Have some cake." Michael handed Dean a paper plate with a thick slice mounded with frosting and a plastic fork on it.

"Thought you'd be off with your friends by now." Dean accepted the cake. He could clearly read the letters *r-a-t* in gold icing on his slice. *How appropriate.*

Michael didn't appear to have noticed, though. "Promised Mom I'd stay until nine, so I've got another half hour." He grinned.

"Well, then, I'm glad I caught you." Should he mention the forgotten gift? No. No point embarrassing them both.

Ten minutes later, the guest of honor had opened his gifts, the cake was eaten, and Dean found himself nursing an iced tea while seated awkwardly on the sofa between Samantha's mother-in-law and sister-in-law. Sam bustled around with a coffeepot and extra napkins. At her insistence, Erica had invited her younger cousins upstairs to her room to braid hair and make friendship pins.

"So...Dean." Jack's dad spoke from an armchair in the corner. "Good of you to come to Mike's grad."

"Wouldn't miss it."

Was that a snort from Sam's direction?

Her father-in-law kindly attempted to continue the conversation. "Samantha tells us you live in Toronto now?"

"That's right." Dean nodded. What to say next? How could someone so comfortable in corporate board rooms feel so out of place in his own sister's home?

The other man valiantly carried the ball. "Have they got all the crops in down there? I imagine they must be knee-high by now."

Dean knew nothing about crops, knee-high or otherwise, but the question reminded him that the senior Mr. Beaudrie was a farmer. "I can't really say for sure. Are they looking good around here this year?"

The question succeeded in keeping the man talking for a full five minutes while Dean tried his best to listen. Eventually, the sister-in-law moved, and Dean slid over to better engage the farmer. He'd stick out the evening, no matter what. A deal's a deal, even if no one in the room knew about the one he'd made. *Stupid traffic light, anyway.*

Michael's grad cards were being passed around, and when they reached Dean, he took his turn flipping through them. The humorous ones brought an honest chuckle. Most leaned toward the serious side. All of them served to remind Dean that he had not brought one and that his pathetic gift lay on his car seat. Served him right for not having enough forethought to get a proper card and put some cash in it.

The last card in the stack made Dean suck in his breath. Instantly, he recognized Marianne's handwriting. He glanced around the room, but no one paid any attention to him. The women gathered around the kitchen island to instruct Jack on the finer points of loading a dishwasher. Jack's brother and father engaged in deep conversation with Michael, who was no doubt counting down the minutes until he was free to go hang out with his friends.

Dean examined the card in his hands. Marianne had chosen a religious one. *Typical.* His ex-wife had always embraced her faith, and Dean had managed to fool her long enough to say *I do.* She'd soon realized he'd only been going through the motions. God was as distant as his own father, probably more. Especially after they lost Anna.

Although it had been painful to hear that Marianne had found a new husband, at least she now had someone who shared her faith. A black man. Even with the added challenge of a mixed-race marriage, Marianne seemed to be making this one work. Dean wracked his brain to recall her new last name. Penny-something? Penning? Pennington, that was it.

The card had a meaningful poem printed inside, but it was Marianne's hand-written words on the left that drew Dean's eye.

Dear Michael,

You know you've always been my favorite boy, right?

Marianne had drawn a little smiley face beside this line.

I am so proud of you, I could burst. I know you've worked hard for this, and I wish you every blessing. God has a special future planned for you, and I see great and wonderful things ahead. I know our paths have not been able to cross often this past decade, but I want you to know I love you and have always been proud and pleased to be your aunt. I won't stop praying for you. Trust in the Lord. He loves you and will be with you wherever you go.

Love,

Aunt Marianne

Dean swallowed hard. His ex-wife had kept up a relationship with his nephew all this time, while he knew next to nothing about the boy. She'd not only given him a thoughtful card, she'd likely enclosed a generous check as well.

What is wrong with me?

Dean passed the stack of cards to Michael's grandfather and excused himself. In the bathroom, he stared at his reflection in the mirror. The rims of his eyes reddened as a film of moisture gathered.

You're a failure, Jacobs. Oh sure, you can shine at work and design gizmos and sell products and fly around the world impressing clients. But you can't even maintain a relationship with your own relatives. Even now, you'd rather be alone with a bottle than here. You're a loser, and you're not fooling anyone.

He splashed some cool water on his face and dried it quickly. When he returned to the main part of the house, the group had become quiet. Jack's dad was speaking.

"This might be our last chance to all be together before the travelers have to return home, so, before you leave, Michael,

I'd love to say a prayer of blessing over you. Would that be all right?"

Dean stood still. Could he get out the front door unnoticed?

"Sure, Gramps." Michael sought the middle of the living room while the adults began gathering around him.

Impossible to get past them without being seen. Dean stepped sideways toward the back door, but before he could reach it, a feminine arm slipped through his.

"C'mon, Dean." Samantha tugged on him. "It'll do ya good."

"Long as I'm not expected to say anything," Dean muttered. He allowed his sister to pull him into the circle, where Michael's grandfather had placed one hand firmly on the young man's shoulder. Others touched Michael's back or arm. Samantha reached out and took her son's hand. Michael didn't resist.

"Let's pray," the farmer said.

Dean found a spot of Michael's shirt that wasn't already claimed by anyone and pinched a bit of the fabric between two fingers.

"Lord," the grandfather began. "Here's your boy, Michael. We know you're proud of him, 'cuz we are. We know you love him even more than we do, 'cuz you made him. You gave him a bright mind, a healthy body. A heck of a sense of humor."

A chuckle rippled through the little circle, and Dean's shoulders relaxed. What would it be like to be in the center of such a huddle, to be the one being blessed?

"We know you have big plans for this young man, and we entrust him to you and pray that you will bless his life with every good thing. Fulfill your purpose in him, God. Now take the rich roots that Jack and Samantha have given him and turn them into powerful wings. Your word says they that wait upon you will rise up and soar like eagles, and we know we'll see that in Michael's life in the years to come. Thank you for this young man. Bless him, Lord. Bless him."

A murmur of *amens* followed as the group moved apart. Samantha grabbed a box of tissues from the counter and passed it around to the women, who all blew their noses and wiped their eyes. The men cleared their throats.

"Thank you, Gramps. Thanks for the party, Mom!" With that, Michael was out the door. Off to a bright, blessed future like the one Dean had squandered.

Chapter Twenty-Three

As Jack had predicted, the sky opened up with rain around the same time Michael left the house. Shortly after, Dean drove back to his hotel with windshield wipers flapping at top speed. He circled the block, not sure he could trust himself to walk through the lobby, past the bar, and go straight to bed. The gathering at Sam's house had helped kill an hour, but it had also stirred up longings in his heart he hadn't allowed himself to feel in a long time. Surely, they needed numbing.

Finally, he pulled into the parkade and turned off the engine. It was too late to find an A.A. meeting. Should he call his sponsor? Rick might be glad to hear from him, but it was an hour later back home.

God, give me strength.

Without stopping to think about it any further, he marched inside and straight across the lobby to the check-in counter.

"Can I help you, sir?" a young woman with a big smile asked.

"Yes. I'm Dean Jacobs. I'm in Room 303."

"Lost your key?"

"No. I requested that the mini-fridge in my room be emptied. Can you please send someone up to ensure it's still empty? I'll just stand here and wait. Thanks."

She stared at him a moment, then turned to the man beside her.

Her co-worker had been listening. "Sir, I can assure you, if you requested that the fridge not be stocked, no one would have—"

"Please send someone to double-check before I go up." Dean spoke as firmly as possible without being rude. "I appreciate it."

"Yes, sir. I'll check myself." He stuck his head around the corner of the office space behind them and spoke to someone, then stepped into the elevator.

Dean hung around the counter, flipping through tourism pamphlets but not really absorbing anything they said. Music thumped from the bar only feet away. The events of the evening kept playing in his head like a CD stuck on repeat. Michael's heartfelt speech about Felicity Gordon. Her "God bless you, Dean" spoken as though she actually, somehow, held the power for God to bless him. Marianne's sincere card to Michael. The farmer's words of blessing on Mike, which his nephew handled with such ease—as though it was a normal part of life. And, most of all, the glaring red traffic light at the intersection of Sophia Street that had directed Dean to his sister's house in the first place.

All of it reminded Dean of what he was missing—and what he would continue to miss if he didn't call his sponsor and get his butt back to a meeting and back to church.

The hotel employee returned with a nod for Dean. "It's all good, sir. Completely empty."

Dean managed to enter the elevator without so much as a glance in the direction of the bar. In his room, he crawled into bed as quickly as he could and fell asleep straightaway. It helped that he was so exhausted.

Sunday morning dawned, still overcast, but no longer raining. Dean was starving. He pulled on some blue jeans and a T-shirt and headed out. Grabbing a breakfast sandwich and coffee from the same deli he'd patronized the day before, he carried it to his dad's apartment atop the puzzle box from his front seat. Inside, he plunked the box onto his father's puzzle table. It had come full circle.

He sat and stared at the box cover while he ate his breakfast. It really was beautiful. How long had Dad had it? Where did it come from? His parents hadn't always enjoyed jigsaw puzzles, but after Mom's stroke, Dad found it was something they could work on together—or, at least, appear to work on together. Mom mostly sat and watched with a glazed-over stare while Dad hunted for the right pieces. He could see how Dad might have taken to the hobby. He had no desire to remember his mother that way, however, and shook his head to chase away the guilt of not visiting her in the nursing home before it was too late.

Turning his attention to the task at hand, Dean found more puzzles among the books. By six that evening, two dozen large, packed boxes lined the walls of the room. He'd labeled them with a black marker—BOOKS, PUZZLES/GAMES, KNICK-KNACKS, PHOTOS. In the center of the room sat six large trash bags filled with old newspapers and magazines, more outdated medication Dean found in the drawer of an end table, two ratty old afghans, numerous small pillows that could no longer be called decorative by anyone's description, and a set of extremely dusty drapes.

Dean took one last look around and gave a firm nod. Tomorrow, they could load up the back of Jack's truck and then clean the place. The puzzle box still lay on the table, the beautiful girl gazing down the wishing well. What did she wish for? Dean had no idea, but for some reason, he couldn't bring himself to add the puzzle to any of the bags or boxes.

When he arrived at the apartment building on Monday morning, Jack's truck waited in the parking lot. Good. Sam was already here. With two coffees and a bag of bagels in his hands, he found the door to Dad's apartment ajar. He pushed it open with one foot.

"Sam?"

"Over here."

Dean followed her voice into the living room where he found his sister at Dad's puzzle table, working on the puzzle.

"You've done a good job in here." She didn't even look up. "Ready to start on the kitchen?"

"Um...sure. Soon as I've had my coffee." He handed her a cup. "Are you kidding me with this puzzle?"

"Thanks." Sam took the cup and lifted the tab. "What do you mean?"

"Who's got time for this? It's going to take us all day and then some to clean out this—"

"I know, I know. Don't get your shorts in a bunch. I just thought I'd look at it while I waited for you, and one thing led to another, and, well...you know I can't resist a nice puzzle."

Dean had not known that, but he let it go. Just as he had no intention of mentioning this puzzle had been a clumsy grad gift for Michael.

"Besides," she continued, "we need to know if all the pieces are here."

"Couldn't you just count them?" Dean reached into the bag of bagels and pulled one out.

Sam followed suit. "Yes, I suppose I could. But where's the fun in that?"

"I don't think any of this is supposed to be fun. I'm glad you're here, though. I've already filled enough bags and boxes to load the truck *twice*—once for the thrift shop and once for the garbage dump."

Sam looked around the room. "Didn't you find *any*thing worth keeping?"

Dean pointed at a box labeled FAMILY PHOTOS. "You might want to take that home. Please don't start going through them now, though."

Sam rolled her eyes and sighed. "I won't."

After hauling the garbage bags down to the truck to create some space, Dean and Samantha rolled up their sleeves to tackle the kitchen. Sam cranked up the radio, switching Dad's favorite talk station to one that played oldies from the sixties and seventies. They laughed and worked their way through the hits of the Osmond Brothers, the Jackson Five, Elton John, and Captain and Tenille. What a difference another person could make. Dishes and silverware were placed in boxes for the thrift shop. Contents of the fridge and pantry were scooped directly into trash bags. At one point, Samantha let out a scream and ran into the living room, where she hopped up on the couch.

Dean got on his knees. A mousetrap lay at the back of the lower cupboard Sam had been cleaning out. A shriveled and dried speck of something on the bait catch indicated it had once been set, but it had long been sprung. And no evidence of a mouse remained. He pulled the trap out of the cupboard and showed it to Sam.

"See? No mouse."

"I don't care. Get it away from me! I can't go back in there."

"Oh brother." Dean tossed the trap into a bag.

Samantha refused to return to the kitchen until Dean had completely cleaned out the lower shelves and promised her he had not found a single mouse dropping.

"It was probably just a precaution," he said.

"Then why was it sprung?"

Dean rolled his eyes, chuckled, and kept working. Sam eventually joined him, but her darting eyes mimicked the very rodent she feared encountering.

Soon enough, they were able to move on to their father's bedroom.

"I already got anything I might have wanted out of here when Mom died, including her jewelry box." Sam started stripping the bed. "So if there's anything you want—say so."

"There's not."

Anything that wasn't thrift shop-worthy went straight into a garbage bag.

At four-thirty, Jack arrived with pizza. After a hasty meal, he and Dean made their first run to the dump while Samantha stayed behind to keep sorting, bagging, and boxing.

"Sure glad you came." Jack kept his eyes on the road ahead.

"Oh?" Dean studied his brother-in-law's fingers as they tapped out a rhythm on the steering wheel. Jack was a man of few words and still fewer encouraging ones—at least, where Dean was concerned.

"It's been real good for Sam to have you here. She hasn't been able to face that apartment, and I was really dreading coming over there just now. But when I walked up the hallway and heard the two of you laughing and music playing, well...I don't think I've heard her laugh like that since your dad's been gone."

"In that case, I'm glad I came too." Dean cleared his throat. "Sure will feel good to have it done."

When they returned, Sam was counting out loud. Dean followed the sound of her voice to the living room. She sat at the puzzle table, putting the pieces into the box once more. She glanced up at him, but the counting only got louder.

"...ninety-seven, ninety-eight, ninety-nine, FIVE HUNDRED! They're all here." She smiled at Dean in triumph. "Can you believe it? They're all here!"

"So you decided to take big brother's advice."

"I'd have loved to finish it, but—there's never enough time, is there?" Her eyes glistened. Was her lip quivering?

"You okay?" Dean stood frozen. Should he offer her the puzzle? Who could understand women?

"Oh, I'm more than okay." Sam held up the puzzle box. "It's just so darn beautiful, this thing, isn't it?"

Dean glanced back at Jack, who stood leaning against the door jamb with crossed arms. Jack shrugged.

"I don't know what it is." Sam's voice broke. "Seeing Mike graduate... knowing he's off to college soon... having you here to help... the relief of finally getting at this nightmare task and not being alone with it... it's everything, really." She let the tears run down her cheeks. "But it's all good."

Dean stepped forward with open arms, and his sister moved into his embrace. "I'm sorry I took so long, Sis. And I don't just mean about this."

She hugged him tight. "Thanks for coming." With a big sniff, she pulled away and wiped her eyes on her sleeve. "Okay. What's next?"

The three of them kept cleaning and emptying the apartment. The laughter dwindled as fatigue set in, but the new warmth remained. Their conversation turned more serious, and while Jack carried a load down to the truck, Dean decided to confide in his sister.

"I admire how you guys have managed to hang onto your faith." He couldn't quite look her in the eye as they finished going through Dad's clothes.

"What do you mean?"

"That prayer that Jack's dad prayed over Michael last night? That was really something. It was obviously not the first time anything like that ever happened. You all seemed right at home with it."

"Yeah. I guess we are. Sometimes, I forget it's not the way you and I grew up. Talking to God as a friend seems so natural now."

Dean nodded. "It shows. I admire that."

"Well, it's not anything you can't have, too, Deano." Sam rolled up a pair of pants and added them to a box of clothes.

Jack returned, and no more was said about God or faith.

"I do believe I've made three decisions this trip." Dean took a deep breath.

Sam studied his face. "Three?"

"Yep. I'm starting a new policy for my life. It's called *One Thing In, One Thing Out.*"

"Every time you bring something new into the house, something else has to go?" Jack asked.

"Exactly. That's the only way I can be sure what happened to Dad doesn't happen to me. In fact, I might start downsizing as soon as I get home."

Samantha lifted another box onto the pile. "And what else?"

"I decided I'm coming to visit you guys more—maybe even when there's no special occasion."

"You better." Jack placed one hand over his heart. "I hope there won't be any more special occasions for a long time. Not sure this ol' ticker can handle it."

"Aww. You old softy." Samantha reached up to rustle her husband's hair. "I can't even muss your hair—it's too mussed already."

Jack ducked out of the way and carried a box into the living room. "That's only two things, Dean. What's the third?"

Dean followed with another box, tempted to think up something different than what he had intended to say. But then he blurted it out. "Soon as I'm home, I'm getting myself to an A.A. meeting. I'm kinda overdue." He made eye contact with Sam. "Hold me to it?"

She nodded. "Sure will."

As they loaded the last of the furniture, Sam lifted the puzzle box and handed it to Dean. "Any chance this will fit inside that container labeled PUZZLES?"

Dean took it and brushed a hand across the top. "Maybe. But I haven't found anything of Dad's I want to keep yet. I think maybe I'll keep this."

Chapter Twenty-Four

Winnipeg, Manitoba. October 1999

*B*ecause you're eighty-six, Uncle Ray, that's why." Pearl plunked the cup of coffee down in front of Ray without bothering to wipe away the drops that splashed onto her oak table. "And because we care about you."

Ray watched her return the coffee pot to its place. She could have been Caroline thirty years ago. Same eyes, same complexion. Same bossy tendencies. "What's my being eighty-six got to do with anything?" He added sugar to his coffee and stirred. And stirred. "I could be *ninety*-six or *a hundred* and six. Makes no difference. I should get to live where I want. And where I want is in the same house where I always have."

"Which is going to fall in on you any moment, and you know it. You can't afford to keep it heated in winter. It's a sweat lodge in summer. And you've got no family left in Wishing Well to watch out for you." Pearl threw a dish towel over one shoulder and started loading the dishwasher.

His niece may have married into the Martindale family, but her spunk was all Caroline.

"You're just like your mother. God rest her soul." Ray made an extra slurpy noise while he drank his coffee just to annoy his favorite niece.

"Thank you. I take that as a compliment."

"Well, anyway, I suppose it's a done deal now, ain't it?"

"Not really, no." With a sigh, Pearl came over to the table and sat down across from Ray. "Your place has been up for sale for eight weeks with little interest expressed. You can change your mind. I just don't think you should. Your family's all here in the city now—what's left of us. Brian and I bought this house and the little one next door in case our kids wanted it. And if they didn't—which they haven't—it would be an investment. But that hasn't worked out all that great. Do you have any idea how hard it is to find good renters?"

Ray shrugged. "What makes you think I'd be a good one?"

"We want you here, we really do. And I think you'll like it if you give it a chance, Uncle Ray."

"And that's another thing. You're forty-eight years old. I really think you could drop the 'uncle' and just call me 'Ray.'"

"That's probably not going to happen, but look." Pearl moved to the window and pulled the blind all the way up so Ray could get a better look at the house next door. "There's a neglected little garden out back, and if that's not enough to keep you busy, you can take care of our yard too." She chuckled.

"Oh, so now the truth comes out. You're lookin' for a slave."

Pearl either didn't hear him or chose to ignore his barb. "You'll love our church. It has an active seniors' group— they're off on day trips at least once a month. They volunteer here and there. You'll make more friends than you ever had in Wishing Well. Especially after the town dwindled to 'population twenty-five.'"

"It's fifty-two."

"Whatever. You can move in this weekend if you want. It's all ready. You can be cozy before winter, and if your place doesn't sell until next year or even the next, it won't matter, because—"

"You'll be able to spy on me."

"—you don't have to pay us any rent!"

Ray cleared his throat. "Doesn't sound like much of an investment."

Pearl let out an exasperated sigh. "Uncle Ray! We love you. We need to know you're—"

"Okay, okay! You can quit yer sales pitch. I'll do it."

Pearl stopped, her hands in mid-gesture. "You will?"

"'Course I will. You had me at, 'Hey, Uncle Ray. Brian and I have an idea.' I just wanted to see if your heart was really in it."

"That's great!" Pearl's face lit up like one of those neon signs he'd seen downtown. She looked so much like Caroline, it almost hurt. "Let me go grab the key, and we can head right over there." She disappeared into the next room.

For the millionth time, Ray thanked God he'd made peace with Caroline before it was too late. He wouldn't have a relationship with his nieces and nephews now if he'd let things continue the way they had for far too long. He may never have met Pearl's kids, Ben and Naomi—the two people who had both Matthews and Martindale blood flowing through their veins.

A photo of himself beside Naomi at her high school graduation smiled back at him from the front of Pearl's fridge.

Look, Sarah. This is our grand-niece, Naomi Martindale. She looks so much like you, it takes my breath away. She's got your beauty and my love for art. Says she wants to go study at some fancy school in Halifax.

Next to the photo hung a pencil sketch Naomi had done from the same picture. According to Pearl, only Naomi shared Ray's artistic talent. She wasn't bad. Ray still studied her sketch, mug in hand, when Pearl returned.

"Hurry up and finish your coffee so we can go see the house."

"Such a pushy one."

Truth be told, Ray had been worried sick about how he'd manage another winter in the old house. Though he enjoyed good health, he couldn't afford to fix the place up, and it wouldn't be worth it if he could. Anybody buying land in the district wasn't looking to live there. Small farms were being swallowed up into large ones. Whoever bought the place would surely demolish the buildings and clear the trees to create a field for crops. In a few years, there'd be no sign that anyone ever lived there. Ray really didn't want to be near enough to witness it. Better to get out completely.

And he indeed felt curious to see the little house next door.

Pearl grabbed a key from a hook. "C'mon, let's go."

It took about thirty seconds to walk from front step to front step.

"Our former neighbor built this house in 1960." Pearl unlocked the door. "We've replaced the shingles and the windows—all five of them. And we ripped out the carpet that used to cover some decent hardwood in the living room and hallway. It could use a good sanding and polishing."

Ray stepped into the little bungalow. Four small rooms plus a bathroom made it seem more like a cottage, but it was all he really needed. A window over the sink in the galley-style kitchen looked out into a fenced backyard with one tree.

"Is that some kind of plum?" The tree was bare now, but its fruit littered the ground beneath.

"Yes. Someone told us they're called Pembina plums."

The sight resurrected memories of his favorite paintings of the old plum tree in all four glorious seasons. "Ought not to let those go to waste," he chastised his niece. "We had one on the farm until some bug managed to kill it."

"Well, when you live here, you can do whatever you want with the plums." Pearl pulled on a drawer handle. "See how easily these drawers slide in and out? And look at this." She opened a lower corner cupboard with a hinged door to reveal a lazy Susan. "You won't have to reach in to get things. I love mine. Use it for small appliances." She gave it a spin.

Ray's only small appliance was a toaster which he always kept handy on the kitchen counter, but he didn't bother to say so. Pearl led him down a short hallway. He stuck his head into the bathroom. White fixtures, not pink or green or even blue like he'd seen in some homes from the same era. *Good.* A small bedroom came next. Its window, too, looked into the backyard and would do nicely.

"And now for the sunny side." Pearl led Ray into the living room, where a three-paned, south-facing window allowed the midday sun to stream into the room and glimmer across the hardwood floor. "We might want to install some blinds for summer, but all the sunlight in here will feel great in winter."

Ray nodded. Through the window, he could see the city street and the houses on the other side. A sidewalk divided "his" small front yard from a boulevard where a fully-grown shade tree flourished.

"I know it'll take some getting used to, living in the city." Pearl tested a light switch. "But it's really a pretty quiet neighborhood."

"I lived in the city once before, you know." Ray put his face close to the window and looked in both directions. "For a little while."

Pearl's voice softened. "Mom told me. I'm sorry you didn't get to finish school."

A sense of peace wrapped Ray like an embrace. "I made the right choice."

Pearl turned and headed into the hallway again. "One more room to see."

Ray followed her as she kept talking.

"It could be a second bedroom, or an office, or...whatever you like." She stopped just inside the room and swept her hand in a wide arc. The same brilliant sunshine poured into this room through a smaller version of the three-paned window. The walls had been painted a cheery yellow with peach tones, a color Ray had once seen labeled *Persian Melon*. The room was empty except for one thing, and when Ray saw it, he stopped breathing for a second.

There, in the corner, stood an artist's easel.

He looked at Pearl.

A brilliant smile lit up her face, and she resembled her mother more than ever. But she said only three words. "Just in case."

By Christmas, Ray was not only settled into the little house but had become a regular fixture at Pearl's church and at the seniors' group. Once a month, they brought a bag lunch and ate together after the service. They'd dig out the old hymnbooks, and Elsie Rogers would bounce on the piano bench, her hands flying up and down the keyboard as they sang. Every fourth Thursday, they went on some sort of outing together. So far, Ray had toured the Manitoba Legislative Building and Lower Fort Garry.

On the Sunday closest to Christmas, the youth group and their leaders served the seniors a full-course turkey dinner. After everyone ate their fill, three of the youth joined Elsie, adding guitars and drums to her lively piano while they all sang Christmas carols until their voices were hoarse. Finally, they stopped for dessert and coffee.

"It's time you joined us at the thrift shop." Mabel Peterson handed Ray a plate.

Several of the women and a couple of the men volunteered at one of the Mennonite thrift shops a few blocks from the church. They organized donations of used clothing and household items to provide affordable goods to those who needed them while at the same time raising funds for local charities and overseas missions. It was a win-win-win venture, but Ray couldn't imagine himself being involved.

"What could an old coot like me do at a thrift shop?" He forked up a bite of his raisin pie.

Mabel leaned toward Ray. "Oh, you'd be surprised. Right, Charlene?"

Another woman took up the cause. "Oh, yes. There's no end of tasks you could do. We're always looking for someone to test and repair small appliances."

"Or sort through bags full of donated items," Mabel added.

"Or sorting and filing reusable price tags."

"Or touching up furniture."

"Or folding plastic shopping bags."

Mabel's husband, Arnold, joined the conversation. "You may as well jump in and say yes. They won't stop until they wear you down." The man had a twinkle in his eye.

"You help out there?" Ray pointed his fork at Arnold.

"I sure do. I'd love another male presence."

And that's how Ray Matthews became a seemingly permanent fixture at the Corner Thrift, helping out two days a week with every conceivable chore.

By the following Christmas, Ray's farm had finally sold.

He'd also produced twelve paintings which Corner Thrift sold at their special events for the tidy sum of twenty dollars apiece. He had never dreamed he'd paint again. But then, he never dreamed he'd have so many friends either. Or that he'd work in "retail," if you could call it that. Or that he'd ever become one of those people whom others looked to for answers—staff, volunteers, and customers alike.

Most of all, he never dreamed he'd find one truly special and thoroughly feminine friend.

Part 5: 2017
Leesha

Chapter Twenty-Five

Winnipeg

Leesha Pennington desired nothing more than to pull her wild black curls into a ponytail and kick around the house in yoga pants and a sweatshirt. But up-and-coming young professionals dare not show themselves in public without being perfectly groomed, not if they hoped to make it in the world of law. And she couldn't afford to stay home, even if it *was* Saturday, her only day to comb the thrift shops for underpriced valuables she could turn around and sell online. Such sales were her only hope of paying off the student loans she'd already racked up getting her pre-law degree and writing the LSAT. She promised herself she wouldn't start law school until she had these debts cleared, just in case the last hurdle failed her—the bar exam.

Bad enough she might be seen at a thrift shop. She didn't have to look the part too.

An hour later, her makeup expertly applied, her hair secured into a neat chignon, Leesha pulled on her third-best pantsuit—a serious navy blue with white piping at the faux pockets—and slipped into the lowest of her high heels. Though running into a co-worker was highly unlikely, one of her firm's clients could spot and recognize her. Leesha took the stairs from her second-floor apartment and headed into the cool April morning.

Winnipeg weather could be so unpredictable this time of year—anything from a late spring blizzard to summer heat. Sunshine and a cool breeze greeted her today.

Leesha opened the door of her 2005 Buick Century. It might be getting rusty around the bottom, and it might not have all the latest bells and whistles, but it was paid for, and it got her where she was going. Dad had taught her well—regular maintenance before you need a repair. And Mom had introduced her to the world of thrift shops when she was still a preschooler. Marianne Pennington was nothing if not frugal. Nearly every outfit and toy Leesha had owned in those early years was pre-owned, if not by a donor to the shop, then a hand-me-down from her much older cousin, Erica. Who, Leesha didn't understand until her teen years, was not truly a cousin at all. Erica was a niece from Mom's first marriage—on her ex's side. Mom had dumped the husband but kept up a relationship with some of his family members, and nobody found it odd. Except for Leesha, once she figured it out.

It explained why Erica wasn't half black, like Leesha.

Leesha had a regular shopping route all worked out, starting at the thrift shop closest to home and looping around to hit up to ten stores in a single Saturday, depending on how much she found. The thrift shop volunteers were getting smarter all the time about which donated items held value, making Leesha's quest more challenging. She'd heard that some of the stores had at least one person whose sole task was to peruse websites, figuring out which items should be separated from the others. Occasionally, they'd put these on a silent auction and sell to the highest bidder. Leesha participated sometimes but was usually outbid.

Her goal was to find those items that somehow slipped past these watchdogs—a Herno raincoat or a Lacoste bag, perhaps—which got hung with the other items going for five to ten dollars.

You had to know what to look for. She'd once found a first-edition copy of L. M. Montgomery's *Anne of Avonlea* that had brought a good price.

And sometimes, you had to be patient. Carefully wrapped in tissue on her closet shelf sat a copy of *Peace with God* signed by the Reverend Billy Graham. Leesha was counting on it becoming a lot more valuable after the man departed this earth to be with Jesus, and how long could she possibly have to wait? He was already ninety-eight. Not that she'd shared her cold-hearted scheme with anyone.

Her biggest find to date had been a diamond ring displayed with the costume jewelry under a sign that read *any ten items for five dollars*. The price she got for the ring had covered three months' rent.

"Don't you ever feel guilty?" Mom had asked her once.

"Why should I?"

"You're getting something for ridiculously less than it's worth. What if someone donated that ring by mistake or lost it?"

Leesha had simply shrugged. "Their loss. Finders keepers." Besides, she'd bought her share of duds, too. She usually donated them back to the store where she found them, so they were even.

But Mom's comment had dampened her enthusiasm for the game. She'd never really thought of it that way before. She pushed the guilt away and concentrated on the challenge of finding potential valuables—although she acquired fewer every month.

She pulled into the parking lot at her first store, the same one she and Mom had shopped at for years. After her tenth birthday, Mom would let her do her own shopping. She'd be given a twenty-dollar bill and could pick out whatever she wanted as long as she understood that was all she'd get and they wouldn't shop again for months. She'd be stuck with her choices—a lesson in real life. Leesha had learned to put together outfits she was happy wearing to school, and she'd learned to grab a brand-name sweater or pair of jeans when the opportunity presented itself. The habits had stuck. Although she no longer shopped here for her own clothes, she never bought anything new. The outfits she found at various high-end consignment shops were perfectly good enough for her job at Rowen, Rowen, and Hyde. In fact, she could confidently say she was the best-dressed paralegal at the firm and that no one would guess the strict limits of her clothing budget.

The thrift shop's familiar old smell assaulted her nose the moment she walked through the door—some unique blend of musty books and old sweat that Leesha had never quite put her finger on and never detected anywhere else. Each store's odor was unique but equally pungent. This one was well-lit and nicely laid out. Leesha knew the floor map and made her rounds of each department. A quick trip down the clothing aisles produced nothing. In the toy department, she spotted an older Barbie doll still in its box. The back side of the box confirmed it was the 1991 Happy Holidays Barbie, priced at five dollars. The right collector would pay much more, so she placed it in her basket. Among the dishes and glassware, a Royal Albert teacup and saucer in the Old Country Roses pattern attracted her notice. A small chip dashed her hopes, and she put it back on the shelf. She had rules.

The books and games department turned up nothing. Leesha never bothered with the small appliances since none were of much resale value. She moved on to the jewelry and picked out a brooch that reminded her of the one in Mom's treasure box. It had been passed down from her grandmother. Maybe Leesha could turn the dollar-fifty for this one into twenty from a nostalgic customer.

She carried the doll and the brooch to the cashier, paid, and carried on to her next stop. By midafternoon, she'd visited six stores, and nine items waited in the trunk of her car. She would spend the evening cleaning everything and taking pictures. On Sunday morning, she'd hunt online before uploading the photos and taking bids. Hunger and fatigue tempted Leesha to skip the last store and go straight home.

"But how will I ever know what I missed out on today?" She pulled into the store's parking lot. She'd allow ten minutes, and if nothing jumped out at her, she'd call it a day. Her yoga pants already called her name.

Corner Thrift had become one of Leesha's favorites. Run almost entirely by senior citizen volunteers who seemed to share a unique camaraderie, the fun, light atmosphere lifted her spirits. Just inside the door, a plump woman with curly gray hair and a colorful spring dress offered her coffee. Her name tag read, *Paula.*

"Oh, no, thanks." Leesha responded automatically even though the coffee smelled awfully good.

"It's Fair Trade," Paula sang, waving the cup around in front of Leesha. "And I can put a lid on it so you don't have to worry about spilling on that beautiful suit. Or on any of our fine merchandise."

"Oh, why not?" Leesha smiled back. "I could use a boost."

"Of course, you could! Cream or sugar?"

"Neither, thanks. Just a lid."

While Paula poured and capped the coffee, Leesha looked off to the side through an open door leading to the back room where donations were sorted and priced. A very old man sat at a table, folding plastic shopping bags into small squares and stacking them into boxes. She found herself staring at the aged hands as they smoothed and carefully handled each bag. She'd read a newspaper article awhile back about a volunteer at one of these stores who had celebrated his hundredth birthday. Was this the store? Could this be the same man? That had been at least a couple of years earlier, though. Surely, the man had passed away by now.

Paula turned and followed Leesha's gaze. She handed Leesha the cup of coffee and leaned toward her as if to share a secret. "That's Ray. He's a hundred and four," she whispered. "Lives in the assisted living facility just down the block—Heritage House. Still comes in three days a week. We'd be lost without him."

Leesha's gut reaction was to say *then you'll soon be lost*, but she only smiled. Why had she never seen the old man before? Perhaps because she'd never stopped to accept a cup of coffee before.

Paula changed the subject. "And if you love the coffee—which you will—we're selling it in five-hundred-gram and one-kilogram bags. Beans or ground, whatever suits your fancy."

"Um...thanks." Buying coffee on these excursions, no matter how Fair Trade it might be, was against Leesha's rules. She moved on, enjoying the coffee as she made her customary rounds through the well-organized departments.

In the toys and games section, her gaze fell on a stack of jigsaw puzzles. Leesha had little appreciation for puzzles and usually ignored them. What was the point? They take a perfectly good picture and cut it into pieces. You put them back together, pat yourself on the back, then take it apart and put it back in the box with nothing to show for your time. How utterly inefficient. If you're going to have a hobby, you should have something to show for it when you're done—like a knitted sweater or some art to proudly display. She'd seen people hang assembled puzzles on their walls, stuck together with some kind of clear overcoat. It made her roll her eyes every time. So tacky.

But another customer was going through the record albums she planned to peruse. While she waited, she may as well look through the puzzles.

Chapter Twenty-Six

The puzzle boxes had not been sorted, so they ranged from twenty-piece pictures of puppies for little kids to thousand-piece photographs of old castles. Two-thirds blue sky made up one of them, and Leesha shuddered to imagine what a nightmare it would be to assemble.

She kept one eye on the record album hog. He needed to move on so she could move in. The guy looked like a leftover hippie from the sixties—rail thin, sandals peeking out from under frayed bell bottoms, a gray ponytail halfway down his back. Probably looking for a *Peter, Paul, and Mary* album. She'd seen a documentary about them recently on YouTube. The man examined the covers and read all the details on the back sides. With a sigh, she moved puzzle boxes from one stack to another, rejecting each one.

Finally, the man picked out a record and headed toward the checkout counter. Leesha put the puzzle she was holding down, and her gaze riveted on the next one in the stack.

It wasn't a photograph, but a painting. A brilliant display of color, the picture featured a beautiful young woman at a wishing well, surrounded by flowers. Carefully, Leesha pulled off the lid. The pieces inside were made of thin wood. Were they all there? She knew little about the value of these old wooden puzzles, except that sometimes the interlocking tabs broke off and created holes in the finished picture even if no pieces were missing. A quick perusal didn't reveal any such breaks. She returned the lid and studied it, captivated by the expression on the girl's face.

What are you wishing for, pretty girl?

Leesha shook her head. She was asking the wrong question. Her rules for Saturday thrift-shopping were clear. Don't stay in one store more than half an hour. Don't buy anything that wasn't in mint condition. Don't over-think. And do not, under any circumstances, purchase anything simply because you like it or want to keep it for yourself. So...was the old puzzle of any value? That's what she should focus on. Probably not. She laid it down again, intending to move on to the records. But somehow, she couldn't stop staring at the image of this innocent-looking girl. What did she see? Would her wish come true, whatever it was? Who was she?

"You want to be careful with that one. Some puzzles refuse to be solved."

Leesha jumped. Her coffee cup fell to the floor as she whirled around. The old man she'd seen folding bags stood a few feet away, watching her.

"Oh, I apologize." He gripped the edge of the puzzle bin. "I'm so sorry. I didn't mean to startle you."

Leesha bent to retrieve the cup and lid. "No harm done. It was nearly empty."

"Paula?" the man called out. "We've got a little spill here."

"No, really, it's okay." Leesha pulled a handful of tissues from her purse and crouched to wipe up the spilled coffee. Then she tucked the tissues into the empty cup and put the lid back on. When she stood again, Paula was there with a wet rag, bending over to give the spot a swipe.

"Oh, I'm so sorry—why don't you let me do that?" Leesha tried to take the rag.

"Already done. Don't you worry about it." With a grunt, Paula stood again. "I'm just glad you didn't add sugar. Sticky stuff."

Leesha looked around for the old man, but he'd disappeared.

"Here, let me take that." Paula held out her hand for Leesha's empty cup. "Would you like another one?"

"Um...no...thank you." How had the man moved so quickly?

"It's good, though, right? Would you like to take a bag home?"

It was the least Leesha could do, even if it meant breaking one of her rules. "Uh...sure." She looked around again. What had the old man meant about some puzzles refusing to be solved?

"I'm thinking a busy gal like you prefers to buy it already ground—am I right?" Paula started back toward the coffee display. "There'll be a bag waiting for you at the cash register whenever you're ready. Take your time."

"Wait." Leesha picked up the puzzle box again. "What did he mean?"

Paula turned. "Who?"

"The man who was standing here when I dropped my coffee. He said I should be careful with this puzzle. What did he mean, and where did he go?"

Paula came closer and leaned in with that conspiratorial look she'd given Leesha before. "Oh, you never know what ol' Ray's going to say. Don't worry about it, love. I'm surprised he wandered out here at all. He usually stays in the back."

"What do you think he meant?"

"Like I said, who knows? Did I mention he's a hundred and four?" Paula glanced down at the box in Leesha's hand. "Oh, that's a pretty one, isn't it? I remember the man who donated it. Said it had been sitting in his closet for years and years. He'd never got around to putting it together, and he was determined to not become a hoarder like his father."

"Do you know if all the pieces are here?"

"You can be sure they were counted before we priced it." To prove her point, Paula rummaged through the other puzzles until she found what she was looking for and held up the castle puzzle that had made Leesha shudder. "See here? This one's clearly marked, *missing a few pieces.* So you can be sure that one's good. Can I ring it up for you?"

Leesha ran one hand gently across the cover of the box. "Sure."

"Mind you..." Paula spoke over her shoulder as she marched toward the cash register. "If it turns out I'm wrong and there *is* a missing piece... we don't give refunds under any circumstances."

Monday morning, as she checked the weather forecast online, Leesha noticed the puzzle lying with the other items she'd brought home from what she liked to call her hunting expedition. The doll and a few other things were already receiving eBay bids, but she couldn't list the puzzle until she knew for sure all the pieces were there and in good condition. That would take more time than she wanted to spend, and she was regretting the purchase.

Invite your parents over.

The thought was as unexpected and nearly as painful as stubbing a toe in the middle of the night. Her parents? Both of them? Mom and Dad had only seen her apartment once, the day they helped her move in. She'd been to their house for Christmas and Easter and maybe a handful of occasions besides that. Usually, Mom called to ask if Leesha wanted some fresh tomatoes from her garden or to say some mail had arrived for her. They didn't hate each other or anything, but they didn't hang out together for the sake of hanging out. They didn't have that kind of relationship.

Steve and Marianne Pennington would likely both drop from heart attacks if their only daughter invited them over for a meal. But they both enjoyed jigsaw puzzles—or they used to. Leesha could remember them pulling her in to help them reconstruct pictures during the Christmas holidays. Leesha would join them long enough to place one piece and then retreat to her room or go out with friends. It had become a joke, them inviting her to help when they knew it wasn't her thing.

When was the last time the two of them had sat down together to do a puzzle—or anything? As far as Leesha could tell, her parents lived two separate lives under the same roof. Besides his job as an engineer, Dad spent every waking moment golfing in summer and watching sports or attending football games, depending on the time of year. He'd had season tickets to the Winnipeg Blue Bombers games for as long as Leesha could remember.

Mom hated sports of any kind. When she wasn't at her job as an administrative assistant, she was involved in some church or charity organization. And when she wasn't doing that, she preferred to be home working in the yard or piecing together quilts. She'd even converted Leesha's old bedroom into a sewing room, monopolized by a big quilting frame. If her parents were ever both home at the same time, Mom would be in the sewing room, working and listening to worship music. Dad would be in the living room, watching a game. They occasionally crossed paths for meals, but Leesha wondered if they even shared a bedroom anymore.

The mental image of the two of them in her apartment, assembling a jigsaw puzzle, nearly made her laugh out loud. Especially since boxes and bubble wrap for shipping eBay purchases filled half her living room. She'd invested in a good scale, measuring tape, and packing tape. But until she moved to a place with a second bedroom, she had no way to keep it out of sight. Entertaining in her home was not a high priority.

Still, she couldn't shake the idea. It would be a practical way to solve her problem—getting the puzzle done quickly so she could turn a profit. But her parents would also see it as a grand gesture in the right direction, a chance for them to spend time with their daughter and get a little glimpse into her life.

Don't over-think it. If she thought about it too long, she'd come up with a hundred reasons not to. Instead, she sat at her laptop and pulled up her email since they were likely to see that before a text. She fired off a message and sent it to both of her parents' accounts.

Hey, you guys, free to come for dinner one night soon? I've got an old jigsaw puzzle that needs assembling. Thursday or Friday are my best nights. I might even cook! Let me know.

She clicked *send* and closed her laptop. "There. Done." She looked at the puzzle box. "See what you've gotten me into?" She regretted the email already, like she knew she would. Now she'd have to clean the apartment, figure out what to cook, shop for groceries, and endure an entire evening with two people who barely spoke to each other. And what if they couldn't complete the puzzle in one night? Would they expect to come back?

What was I thinking?

Chapter Twenty-Seven

By mid-morning, two separate replies from Leesha's parents arrived. Dad had tickets to the game on Friday night but would love to come on Thursday. Mom said she was teaching a cooking session at the young parents' resource center where she volunteered on Thursday evening. Friday would be perfect.

"I knew I'd regret this." Leesha tossed her phone into her desk drawer and returned her focus to her computer screen. She was supposed to be proofreading a divorce contract for her boss, the *Hyde* in *Rowen, Rowen, and Hyde*. But concentrating on the finer points of the document only brought her parents to mind repeatedly. Why were they still together? On her mother's part, Leesha suspected the shame of having divorced once before prevented her from dissolving her current marriage. She didn't want the stigma of being a twice-divorced woman, especially among her church friends. For Dad, continuing in a lifeless marriage probably trumped living alone or trying to start over with someone new.

By the time she returned to her apartment, Leesha had lost track of how many calls, emails, and texts had gone back and forth trying to find a night that worked for everyone. In the end, Dad would come for dinner on Thursday, and Mom would join them after she finished with the young parents, around eight. On Friday night, Mom would come over to share leftovers with Leesha and, hopefully, finish the puzzle.

Thursday came quickly.

I can't believe I've tied up two evenings of my life for this stupid puzzle. Leesha slid the pan of frozen lasagna into her oven. If the puzzle turned out to be intact and brought in a good price, though, it would be worth it. How weird would it be, trying to make one-on-one conversation with Dad?

He arrived right on time. Dad's black, wooly hair had gone from gray at the temples to white all over, contrasting all the more with his black skin. "Smells great in here!"

"Thanks." She lit the fat candle on her little kitchen table and filled their water glasses.

Dad took the chair Leesha usually used.

She sat across from him. "My table's so small, maybe it's a good thing we're doing this in shifts. I hadn't really thought of that when I invited you both."

"Oh, it would be a little cozy, but we'd have made it work." Dad smiled and folded his hands. "Want me to say grace?"

"Sure." Leesha bowed her head and sent up her own silent prayer while Dad gave thanks for the meal. *God, help me out here.*

Dad delivered his usual meal-time prayer, tacking on a "thanks for this time together," and the two of them managed to make small talk while they ate. *Work was good. Weather is warmer than usual for this time of year. Could use some rain. How 'bout them Bombers?*

When they finished the meal, they carried their coffee mugs into the living room where the puzzle box lay on a folding table next to the floor lamp. "I wanted to have the pieces all laid out, but I ran out of time." Leesha opened the box.

Dad followed and took the lid from her. He stood there, examining it. "Well, I don't know if I've ever done one this old. I'd say it pre-dates colored photography, eh?"

"I'm sure of it. They quit making these wooden ones shortly after World War II, from what I can gather. Hope it's not too girlie for you."

"Well, I do prefer a good picture of a ballgame or a nice green golf course." Dad chuckled. "But if it'll help you out, I can look for pieces on this one just as well." He quickly began sorting the border pieces. "Remember the one with all the dogs? Back in the nineties?"

Leesha rolled her eyes. "Oh, do I! I was just a little kid, but I hated that thing."

"Hardest puzzle I ever saw. Two-sided, with the same picture on both sides."

"Yes. One of them a quarter-turn from the other. And there must have been thirty or more dog faces, all different breeds." Leesha shuddered. "I did my famous find-one-piece-and-run-away trick."

Dad shook his head, reminiscing as he continued to work. "We finished it, though. Your mother and I."

Leesha jumped at this opening but kept her eyes focused on the puzzle. "How are you and Mom doing?"

"How are we doing? You mean, like, health-wise? We're fine. I had a physical just last month. Everything's good. Your mom's good."

Leesha nodded. "Good. Glad to hear it. Um...what about as a couple?

"As a couple?"

"Yeah. How's your relationship?"

Dad neatly fit a side piece to the corner piece. "Well, we don't work on puzzles together anymore, if that's where you're going with this."

"Why not?"

"Oh, I don't know. I guess life just got too busy. You know how it is." He had already finished the right-hand side of the frame and reached the bottom corner.

"Do you guys fight?"

"Fight? No, we never fight."

How much to press? "Do you two do *any*thing together? Go anywhere?"

"Mmm." Dad's bottom lip protruded—considering her question or concentrating on the puzzle? "Church on Sundays."

Leesha usually made it to church on Sundays, too, so she knew her parents were always there, seated side by side. Did Dad really think that constituted a marriage? "And…. what else?"

"Oh, you know … we do stuff."

"Together?"

"Sure."

"Like what? Name something."

Dad rubbed his chin but kept his eyes on the task before him. "Well, we went to that movie—what was it? The Christian one, with the boy and the angel and the—"

"Dad, that was nearly two years ago!"

He looked at her over the top of his glasses. "Really? Seems like—"

"—and you were with a group. When's the last time you and Mom had a date?"

"Honey, what's all this about? Has your mother been talking to you?" Dad was beginning to sound defensive.

"No, no, no, nothing like that." She'd better back off. "Hey, look, I found one." She finally placed her first piece of the puzzle in.

"So that's it? You gonna quit now?" Dad teased. "Leave it for your mother and me to finish?"

"Oh, I think I'm good for another piece or two." Leesha paused. "Sure is a pretty picture, isn't it? Who do you suppose this is?"

Dad looked at the finished picture on the box cover and shrugged. "Probably just a Fig Newton of someone's imagination." He chuckled at the joke Leesha had heard multiple times from him. Then he surprised her by picking up the previous topic. "Leesha, if you're worried about your mother and me, don't. We get along all right. It's just that we each have our own interests—you know that."

"And that's enough for you?"

"Well, sure. I guess. What else is there?"

"Is that how Mom feels too? That you 'get along all right,' and that's good enough?"

Dad took off his glasses and held them up to the light to examine the lenses. He blew something away from the surface and returned them to his face. "I don't know. Why don't you ask her?"

"Seems like something *you* should be asking her. Don't you think?"

"Ha! There you are." He picked up a puzzle piece that showed the girl's hair and one eye and snapped it into place. Then he glanced up at Leesha before concentrating once more on the puzzle. "Didn't realize I was coming over here to be interrogated."

Leesha sighed. "Sorry. Didn't mean to make you uncomfortable."

They worked in silence for a while. Thankfully, she'd thought to put some music on earlier. Soft piano notes of Liszt's "Love Dream" filled the gap. She snuck a peek at the clock. How long until Mom showed up?

Dad must have noticed. Or read her mind. "Oh, you're probably right. I should be asking your mother those kinds of questions. It's just a lot easier to avoid them, you know?"

Leesha didn't know. She'd never been married. Never even shared an apartment. She'd had a roommate in college, but that was different. And she'd had a few boyfriends over the years, a few breakups. None that really broke her heart. She couldn't imagine continuing an empty relationship. What was the point?

"Why, though? Why is it easier?"

"I don't know. Less conflict, I guess. Nobody likes to talk about that kind of stuff."

Leesha shook her head. "I don't believe that. I mean, I'm no expert. But shouldn't married couples be comfortable enough to talk about their feelings?"

"Oh, she's got her girlfriends for that."

"And you?"

"Men don't really do feelings."

Leesha wanted to jump all over that one but paused long enough to let Dad realize what he'd said.

His brow furrowed. "I mean, we don't *share* them. Not that we don't *have* them."

"Uh-huh. So…men don't need to share them. Is that what you're saying?"

"Well, not as much as women."

Leesha cocked her head to one side. "It doesn't bother you that Mom might be sharing personal things with her friends that you know nothing about?"

"I never said that. It's just—oh, I don't know. It's a little scary, I guess. Easier to avoid."

Leesha drained her coffee mug and studied her father. He was a good man. Smart. Respected. Not what you'd call highly ambitious, maybe, but not a workaholic either. If the worst you could say about him was that he was addicted to sports and reluctant to share things on an emotional level, it didn't make him a villain. It probably only made him like ninety-five percent of the male population.

I'd rather stay single.

"What are you afraid of, Dad? Finding out something you don't want to know?"

He paused to consider this. "Maybe."

"Like what?"

She really didn't expect an answer. Her engineer father had nearly completed the entire frame of the puzzle, and the girl in the center quickly took shape. Leesha had contributed maybe five pieces. She was about to go to the kitchen for more coffee when Dad surprised her yet again.

"To be honest? Sometimes, I'm afraid to find out your mother's still carrying a torch for Dean Jacobs."

Leesha sank back into her chair and stared at him. All she really knew about Mom's first husband was that he drank too much and that she had finally left him. And that they'd lost a child, a little girl, hours after birth. Before Leesha could respond, a light tap at the door interrupted their conversation.

Mom's voice rang out cheerfully. "Hello? I'm here!"

Chapter Twenty-Eight

"Mom!" Leesha rose from her seat. Just before heading to the kitchen, she put one hand on Dad's shoulder and whispered close to his ear. "Dad, you *have* to ask her about Dean Jacobs."

She gave Mom a warm smile. "Just in time for dessert!"

"Oh, thanks, sweetheart, but I couldn't eat a thing." Marianne Pennington removed her jacket and threw it over a kitchen chair. "I'll take a cup of that coffee, though."

"You bet." Leesha pulled down her favorite turquoise *Pioneer Woman* mug and filled it. "Want to try some hazelnut creamer in it?"

"Sure. Thanks." Mom moved to the puzzle table.

Mom said "hi" without looking at Dad. He replied without looking at her too. How did they do that? And how was Dad feeling about the bomb he'd just dropped in Leesha's lap? Was he right? Did Mom still love Dean Jacobs? Surely not. Mom hadn't had anything to do with her ex-husband in as long as Leesha could remember—other than staying connected with Dean's sister and her kids. And that, too, had dwindled in recent years.

She handed Mom the coffee.

"Looks like you've made some good progress. What a gorgeous puzzle."

"Isn't it?" Leesha sat and began searching for a piece that would have the girl's hand in it. "And you know me. Not a big puzzler."

"That's the understatement of the year." Mom grinned. "I gotta admit, I was shocked when you told me what you had in mind for this evening."

"Yeah, well…it's all about resale value. I almost missed it." Leesha recounted her experience at the thrift store with the spilled coffee and how she ended up looking at the hated puzzles. She told them about the old man and what he'd said.

"'Some puzzles refuse to be solved'?" Mom wrinkled her forehead. "Whatever did he mean?"

Leesha shrugged. "I don't know. I sort of assumed he somehow knew there were pieces missing, which is why I wanted to assemble it before I try to sell it. Or—I don't know—maybe he had some type of dementia. But if that's the case, how could he be helpful at the store? Apparently, he's there two or three days a week. Has been for years."

"He's really a hundred and four?" Dad raised his brows.

"So they said. Seemed pretty spry to me, though."

Mom was piecing together a section of green ivy that worked its way around the stone base of the wishing well. "I'm not sure I want to live that long. I bet he's lost so much. People who get that old have often outlived their children. I think that would be awful. Imagine the heartaches you'd accumulate in that many years."

"That's one way to look at it, I guess." Leesha sighed. "But think of the wisdom you could accumulate too."

"Just think." Dad put in another piece. "He would have probably been an adult already when this puzzle was made."

After ten minutes or so without finding a single piece, Leesha stood. "My eyes are starting to cross. You two keep going if you want. I'm going to tidy up the kitchen."

"Slave driver," Dad muttered.

Leesha ran hot, sudsy water into the sink and tried to eaves-drop on her parents while she washed dishes. She even turned the music down a couple of notches. At first, they didn't speak at all. Then Dad asked how Mom's evening had gone. Mom talked about the young parents, how little they knew about parenting, and how cute the kids were. How she wished she could do more for them, maybe pull their eyes away from their phones long enough to engage with their children.

When Leesha pulled the plug in her sink, the slurping noise muffled something Dad said, then they both chuckled. She wiped the countertop, straining to listen. Dad was telling a funny story about something that happened at work. They both burst out laughing. She had not heard that sound in so long, she looked for reasons to stay in the kitchen. She began wiping down the stove, then the handle on the fridge door, then the inside of the microwave, hoping to hear that laughter again.

Finally, she wandered back into the living room. "Wow, look at you guys go!" The puzzle was really taking shape, the girl nearly complete. A profusion of flowers and blue sky were all they had left.

Dad stretched and yawned. "Well, I'm about done. Think you two can finish this tomorrow night?"

"I guess we'll see." Mom put in one more piece. "I'm done-in for tonight too. Thanks so much for this, Leesha. I'd forgotten how much I enjoy a good puzzle."

"Hey, don't thank me. Thank *you*!"

"You gonna give us a cut if you make a big profit?" Dad shrugged into his jacket.

Leesha grinned back at him. "Maybe another dinner."

Friday evening, Mom was sitting in her car when Leesha pulled up to her apartment building.

"You been waiting long?" Leesha grabbed her oversized handbag from the back seat and closed the door with one hip.

Mom climbed out and leaned against her driver-side door. "Nope. Just got here. Came straight from work. I've been thinking about that lasagna all day, though. Hope you two had lots leftover last night."

"Oh, there's plenty." Leesha unlocked the door and they went inside, then took the stairs up a flight to her apartment.

"Make yourself at home, Mom. I'm gonna change into sweats."

Mom rattled around in the kitchen while Leesha pulled on her favorite comfy pants and hoodie. When she came out of her bedroom, the microwave whirred with a plate of leftover lasagna, and Mom chopped veggies for a salad.

"Oh, my goodness, Mom! This is supposed to be my treat. You should relax."

"I told you—I'm hungry. You can set the table."

With a sense of déjà vu from the previous night, Leesha lit the fat candle again. With Mom, though, conversation came a little more naturally. As they ate, they chatted about their day and their plans for the weekend. Leesha anticipated another thrift-store outing. Mom hoped to start her spring garden cleanup if the weather cooperated.

"I'm thinking of putting it all to flowers this year. No veggies. Well, maybe just for eating fresh. I'm too old to be fooling around with canning and freezing."

"May as well have something pretty to look at all summer," Leesha agreed.

"Yes, and it will give me a photo opportunity for the quilt I want to make next winter. Working on that flowery puzzle of yours inspired me. There are sweet peas in that picture, which I've always wanted to grow but never have."

"Speaking of which, we should get at it before we're too tired to finish." Leesha picked up their coffee mugs. "I'll pour us both a fresh cup."

Mom moved to the puzzle table, calling out over her shoulder. "Your father asked me the strangest question last night."

"Oh?"

Mom clicked on the lamp over the table and took a seat. "I wondered if you might've had anything to do with it."

Leesha handed her the coffee and sat down. "Well, now I'm really curious."

Mom took a sip before setting her coffee on a coaster. "He wanted to know if I was still carrying a torch for Dean Jacobs."

Leesha's throat went dry. How should she respond? Should she play dumb or admit what Dad had confided? Safest bet—echo her mother's words. "'Carrying a torch?'"

"Yeah. It means ... still in love with or ... I don't know ... holding out hope for or—"

"Yeah, I know what it means."

"Any idea where that's coming from?" Mom found a puzzle piece and snapped it into place.

Leesha focused on the puzzle. "He may have mentioned it."

"You two were talking about me?"

"Not exactly. I asked how the two of you were doing, that's all. Seems you don't spend any time together anymore, and it makes me wonder what kind of relationship you have."

Mom leaned back in her chair and wrapped both hands around her mug. "Who brought up Dean?"

Leesha tried to recall details of the conversation as she fit two more puzzle pieces together. "He did. I think it's been a fear of his, maybe from the start."

Mom let this sink in as she silently kept working.

"So what did you say?" Leesha asked.

"Oh, I immediately denied it. Told him he was crazy for suggesting such a thing."

Leesha studied her face. "But...?"

"But...then it started niggling at me."

"And?" Leesha tilted her head.

"I'm actually glad he asked. It's caused me to do some soul-searching." Mom reached across to Leesha's side of the puzzle and pointed at an empty hole where the piece in her daughter's hand belonged. "I'm not in love with Dean, but I can see where I may have given your father cause to fear."

"Really? I've never heard you even mention Dean's name. Well, almost never."

"No. I think I've worked hard to avoid it. But the fact is, Dean was my first love. We had a child together and lost her, as you know."

Leesha had been ten years old when she first learned about the baby who lived only a few hours. After her mother told her about Anna, Leesha wondered what it would be like to have a big sister.

"That must have been so hard." She couldn't imagine it.

"When you go through something like that with some-one...well, we didn't handle it in a healthy way. Obviously. But still, there is a bond between you. A strong one. I will always care about Dean, what happens to him. I loved his family, and I think my staying in contact with Samantha may have looked like an attempt to stay connected with Dean. I had to ask myself if it was."

"Do you think so?"

Mom sighed and sat back in her chair. "I don't know, honey. Maybe at first—before your dad came along."

"And since then?"

"When I'm honest with myself, I have to admit, I've wasted far too many hours wondering what might have happened if I'd hung in there with Dean. Especially after your dad and I started drifting apart."

"But then you wouldn't have had me." Leesha leaned back in her chair and folded her hands.

"Precisely. And I thank God for you every day, sweetheart."

"But not for Dad?"

Mom shrugged and let out another long sigh. "Sometimes—honestly, I see him sitting there on the couch watching hockey, and I just—well, to say *dislike* him would be putting it very mildly."

"Hate?"

Mom put down her mug and clasped her fingers together. She stared at the puzzle, her lips twisting. "There's a fine line between love and hate sometimes."

Chapter Twenty-Nine

eesha let out a snort and shook her head. "See, this is why I'm not married. It's just way too confusing."

"Your grandparents on both sides warned us that being a mixed-race couple would be challenging, but we've never thought we had any more challenges than anyone else." Mom shrugged. "Maybe we have. I don't know."

"In this day and age, I don't believe that makes much difference, Mom." Leesha folded her arms. "I certainly hope not, anyway. So...when you see Dad on the couch, what do you wish he were doing instead?"

"That's just it. Why does it bug me so much? It's his life to spend how he chooses. And it's not like he's out drinking or gambling or running around with other women."

"True. But still. We all want more out of a relationship. Why doesn't he?"

Mom snapped in another puzzle piece. "I long for him to help out in the yard, for us to work together. I figure it's his yard, too, right? He should take pride in it. Oh, he'll mow the grass if I press, but that's it. The rest is up to me. He just doesn't care about it like I do."

Leesha could empathize with her but also wanted to defend Dad. "It's just not his thing."

"Exactly. And one day, it occurred to me that maybe expecting him to care about the garden would be the equivalent of him expecting me to get enthused about football." She shuddered.

Leesha laughed. She'd respond the same way. "And you weren't prepared to do that?"

"Heck, no."

Leesha chuckled again. "So ... you just settled?"

"I guess I did. And so did he."

"That's so sad."

"Well ... I still feel pretty disappointed, if I'm honest."

"No kidding. Who wouldn't? Do you still feel hatred sometimes?" And did Dad hate Mom sometimes too?

Mom took another swallow of coffee and stared over the top of her cup, elbows resting on the table. "Resentment is probably a better word. Envy, sometimes. I know several women who are on their second marriage, and it's turned out so well for them. Or it appears to have, anyway. They talk like they've finally found their soulmate, and they're so in love, and blah, blah, blah. I guess I wonder why that didn't happen for me, and if I start thinking about it too hard, I have to blame myself. It's much easier to blame your dad."

"Does he know how you feel?" Leesha kept her eyes on the puzzle, hoping to keep Mom talking.

"He doesn't know all of that. But, just before we drifted off to sleep last night, I apologized for giving him cause to worry."

"You did?"

She nodded. "I told him I wanted to work harder at connecting with him. Actually ... and you'll find this funny ..." She chuckled.

"What?"

"Working together on this puzzle last night reminded me—both of us, I think—how much fun we have when we're solving them together. We talk and laugh while we're working.

However frivolous, it gives us a common goal. I don't know why we ever stopped. I honestly cannot think of one solid reason why we stopped."

Their pastor had delivered a message on marriage a few weeks ago. Being single, Leesha had mostly tuned out, but one particular piece had stuck. "I think I do. Remember what Pastor Gene says? 'The devil loves nothing better than to destroy marriages, because if he can do that, he can destroy—"

"—families, which destroys communities, which destroys countries, which destroys the world.'" Mom stretched her arms above her head. "Yes. And he's right."

"So if the enemy sees something in your relationship that's working in your favor, he's going to do everything in his power to bring that thing to an end."

Mom leaned forward until her midsection pressed against the table's edge. "And we don't even see it. Hard to imagine that something so simple as working on a silly jigsaw puzzle could be spiritual warfare."

"No wonder it's a battle. How did Dad respond?"

"He didn't say much. But this morning, he stopped to kiss me before we left for work. Can't remember the last time that happened."

A sudden knock on the door pulled them both out of the reflective moment. Leesha went to answer it, wondering who would be knocking on her door on a Friday evening—or any evening—unexpectedly. She pulled it open.

"Dad!"

Dad stood grinning at his only daughter, one hand behind his back. "Hi there. Am I on time for dessert?"

Leesha stammered. "Um...there might be a little ice cream in the freezer."

"Steve?" Mom had come up behind her. "What's going on? Why aren't you at the game with Bruno?"

Dad stepped inside and pulled a plastic clamshell container out from behind his back—holding half a dozen huge, chocolate chip cookies from Leesha's favorite bakery.

"This," he announced, "is dessert." He turned to his wife. "Bruno's son is in town. He tried to get an extra ticket but couldn't. He was going to give his away, so I said, 'why don't you take *my* ticket and take your son to the game?' He took me up on it."

"Are you serious?" The shocked look on Mom's face was priceless. "You gave away your ticket? Just *gave* it away?"

Dad beamed as though he'd just made a hole in one. "Just gave it away."

Leesha took the cookies from him. "No way, Dad. You never miss a game, and you certainly never give away a perfectly good ticket."

"Never say never. Because I did. Now get me a cup of something hot to go with one of those cookies, and let's get back at that puzzle." He threw his jacket over the back of a kitchen chair and moved to the living room, leaving his wife and daughter standing there.

Mom peered after him, her eyes unblinking and her face slack.

"Alrighty, then." With a soft chuckle, Leesha turned to plate the cookies and start a fresh pot of coffee. When she was done, she joined her parents at the puzzle table. The picture neared completion, and hope rose that all the pieces might indeed be there. "Getting you two over here to work on this thing might just be the smartest move I ever made."

The three of them kept working, talking, laughing, and enjoying the cookies. Leesha checked the clock.

"Game's starting, Dad. Want me to turn on the radio so you can hear it?"

He considered. Then he looked at Mom.

"It's okay with me if you do." Mom shrugged.

Dad blew air through his lips. "No. Don't bother. I'll hear all the details from Bruno soon enough. Wouldn't want to deprive him of telling it." He returned his focus to the puzzle.

Mom's eyebrows rose halfway to her hairline. Leesha suppressed a smirk.

Dad leaned into the table. "Well, come on. Don't sit there staring at each other. Let's get this little lady finished!"

At the Heritage House assisted living facility, Nurse Darseen Braun was making her bedtime rounds. As she neared Ray Matthews' suite, his niece stepped into the hallway carrying a laundry basket filled with Ray's clothes and towels.

"Good evening, Pearl."

Pearl looked up. "Hi, Darseen." She held the door open instead of closing it. The woman must be approaching seventy herself, but she faithfully cared for her hundred-and-four-year-old uncle.

Darseen smiled. "How's he doing tonight?"

"He was quiet. Seemed a little more tired than usual, but what can you expect?"

"He's a marvel, isn't he? Is he asleep?" Darseen peered past Pearl into the tidy suite.

"Yeah. I hung around for a bit. Thought he might wake up again, having gone to bed so early. But I just checked, and he seems to be having himself a really good sleep. Snoring away. Wish I could sleep so peacefully."

"Don't we all?" Darseen waited for Pearl to head down the hallway before entering her patient's suite.

At one minute before ten, Leesha glanced at the clock. She'd never stayed engaged with a jigsaw puzzle this long in her life. The cookies were eaten, the coffee cups drained. By now, they were convinced the puzzle had all its pieces, and the excitement to finish intensified.

"I feel like we should have a countdown," Mom suggested.

Five pieces remained. Dad put one in. Then Leesha. Then Mom. Then Dad.

The three of them stared at the one remaining hole. Clearly, the last piece would fill it—but who would get to do the honors?

"Go for it, Leesha." Dad winked. "You know you want to."

"Given my history, I hardly deserve this. But thanks." Leesha picked up the last piece. With as great a fanfare as she could, she pressed it into place.

All three of them admired the beautiful girl at the wishing well and cheered.

"Woo-hoo!" Mom looked at her watch. "We're done, and it's only ten o'clock."

"With one minute to spare." Dad grinned like a little kid.

Pearl had left a small lamp burning in the living area of Ray's suite. Half a dozen of the man's paintings graced the walls—landscapes, flowers, old farm equipment. Darseen had admired them numerous times, always asking why he no longer painted.

"Quit at ninety-five," he'd told her with a twinkle in his eye. "Gotta leave something for the younger folks to paint. Pearl's girl, Naomi, for example. You heard of her? Naomi Martindale? That one's got talent. Makes big money with it. I'll introduce ya when she comes home from Halifax for a visit."

Expecting to hear his familiar snores, Darseen paused in the archway that separated Ray's bedroom from the rest of the suite.

She listened. Not a sound. She approached the bed. She couldn't even hear him breathe.

"Mr. Matthews?" She took his wrist in her hand and positioned her finger to feel for a pulse. "Ray?"

Darseen checked her watch, then tried again. No pulse. No breath. And his *Do Not Resuscitate* order had been signed.

At one hundred and four years of age, Ray Matthews had passed away peacefully in his bed. Darseen pulled out her notebook to record it. Time of death, nine fifty-nine p.m.

Chapter Thirty

Marianne Pennington pulled her phone out of her purse and took a photo of the finished puzzle. "This picture would make a fabulous quilt, wouldn't it? If I get started on it now, maybe I'll complete it before I die." She laughed.

"Don't forget, you'll be retired in three more years." Dad stretched and spoke over a yawn. "Plenty of time to work on it then."

"True enough. I still need to start on it, though—before the inspiration leaves me."

Leesha snapped several pictures of the completed puzzle from different angles, then began carefully disassembling the puzzle and returning it to its box. "See, this is why I've never really appreciated puzzles. Now it all goes back into the box, and we just lost two evenings of our lives."

Dad's jaw dropped and he let out a mock gasp. "How can you say *lost*? We were together, weren't we?"

"Okay, I'll give you that. It's been good to spend time with you guys. Thanks for helping me. I hope I can get a good price for this thing. I'm listing it tonight."

Her parents hugged her as they said their goodbyes. "Thanks, sweetheart," Mom whispered. "You've done more than you know."

Leesha locked the door behind them and went straight to her laptop. She listed the puzzle for auction to close on Wednesday and uploaded the five best photos. Then she promised herself not to look at it again until Monday. She folded the puzzle table and put it away, reflecting on the time with her parents. It seemed something had been rekindled for them and for that, she was grateful. She laid the puzzle on her kitchen table and turned off the lights, planning to head for bed.

Instead, she returned to her computer and opened it again. She pulled up Google and typed in *Dean Jacobs*. There were too many hits to count, but a Facebook profile looked like it might be him. She'd never met the man, but she'd seen photos—one from the day he married Mom, another of him sitting beside Mom as she held their newborn nephew, Michael. Would Leesha recognize him from those snippets of memory?

It was easier than she'd imagined. Dimpled chins must have been a highly dominant trait in that family. Michael and his mother both had them. The Dean Jacobs she now considered had one too. She clicked on his profile.

Judging by his Facebook page, Dean Jacobs was practically a celebrity. Over ten thousand friends. Photos of him posing with children in developing nations on humanitarian trips. A whole album from his retirement party, including a video where people extolled his virtues. Could this be the alcoholic her mother had divorced?

Leesha was beginning to doubt she'd found the right guy when she came across a picture of him posing with his sister—whom Leesha knew as "Aunt Sam"—and her kids at Samantha's fiftieth birthday party. Though she hadn't seen Michael and Erica in years, she'd recognize her "cousins" anywhere.

So Dean had turned out to be an all right guy, if Facebook proved anything. The man did not appear to have a family of his own. No wife, not even a girlfriend. Seemed like he spent his life traveling and planning fundraisers for worthwhile charities. He served on the boards of several.

Then something he'd posted just six weeks earlier caught her eye. "18 years sober today. Praise the Lord!"

Well, good for him.

Apparently, he also maintained a blog. When a link to his site came up, Leesha clicked on it. The title of the most recent post—six weeks ago—read, "How an Old Jigsaw Puzzle Taught Me a Life Lesson." When the photo that went with it came up, Leesha blinked and cried, "No way."

The puzzle looked exactly like hers—well, not the puzzle, but the box. She retrieved the box from the kitchen and brought it back to her computer to compare.

"What on earth—? How many of these did they make? Must have been pretty common for us to both find the same one." Leesha's hopes of making a bunch of money on the puzzle began to fade. She started reading Dean's story.

My father was a hoarder.

When he passed away, it fell on my sister and me to clean out his apartment, crammed from floor to ceiling with enough stuff to fill ten apartments. Most of it went straight into a dumpster, and that's when I determined my life would not end up like his. The one possession of his that I saved was an antique jigsaw puzzle. I don't know why. It held no nostalgia from my childhood. I don't know where Dad got it. It was half finished when I found it in his living room, and there was something about the unfinished-ness of it that spoke to me. My sister counted the pieces to make sure they were all there, and I took it home to my huge house in Toronto where I stuck it in a closet.

Fifteen years later, when I decided to move back to Winnipeg, the puzzle was still sitting in the closet. Never assembled, not even attempted. It mocked me. Why was I hanging onto something that could bring others joy? Still, I couldn't let it go.

It wasn't until I unpacked my belongings in my new, much smaller place that a clearer head prevailed. I remembered my promise of years earlier—to always get rid of one thing for any new thing I brought home. That's when I packed up the puzzle—along with several other things— and took it all to a thrift shop.

Whether the girl at the wishing well got her wish, I'll never know. But I'm simplifying my life and loving it.

Could Leesha truly have purchased Dean's puzzle at Corner Thrift? What a crazy coincidence. Should she show her mother or not? Did Mom have any idea Dean was back in Winnipeg?

On Saturday morning, Felicity Gordon filled a thermos with hot chocolate and followed Reggie to the car. They were picking up Dan bright and early. The Lord had given them a cool, sunny day for spring cemetery cleanup.

At seventy-five, Reg bragged that he was more mobile than his older brother and a much safer driver. Dan's wife had died the year before, and they started with her grave. There wasn't much to do. The earth was still settling, and it was too early to plant flowers. They quickly moved on to Felicity's parents' graves, where they spent an hour cleaning up dead leaves and scrubbing down headstones.

Then they moved to the grave of Reggie and Danny's mother. While the brothers worked and reminisced, Felicity relaxed in a lawn chair and sipped hot chocolate.

"Remember the radio?" Reggie paused to lean on his rake.

Dan chuckled. "Oh boy. I sure do. That thing lasted for years. Probably the best bargain we ever made."

"And I don't think Mum ever did miss that puzzle."

"What in the world are you boys talking about?" Felicity wiped hot chocolate from her fingers with a tissue. "What radio? What puzzle?"

"Did I never tell you that story?" Reg launched into a tale about an old-fashioned puzzle they'd received for Christmas from their grandparents one year, how it never got completed because of their stubbornness. How they broke their mother's precious radio and ended up pawning the puzzle without her knowledge. How they learned a lesson in paying attention to their mother's needs.

"We could be such scoundrels." Dan shook his head. "Poor Mum."

Felicity smiled. "Well, the two of you did all right. You both ended up investing your lives in young people. I'm sure your mother would be very proud of both her boys."

Dan blushed at the compliment. "That puzzle was too girlie for us, anyway, wasn't it? Some girl at a wishing well. All flowery and so on. Mum liked it, though."

Reggie nodded. "She knew about old puzzles because she once worked for a company that made them. It was wooden. Probably bring in a good price now if we'd hung onto it."

Something in Felicity's memory bank clicked. "Sounds like a puzzle my mother had. Did the girl have brown hair, with flowers in her hair too? Sweet peas, I think, and green ivy wound around everything?"

"Yeah, that sounds like it." Dan packed down the grass, leaves, and twigs in his bag.

"Must have been a popular one." Felicity tried hard to remember the picture. "The girl had the most pensive expression, so you just wanted to stare at her. I remember it because I was determined to finish it before taking it apart and donating it to Mom's care home. That puzzle taught me a lesson in patience. If I'd waited one more day, I'd have finished it."

"Really?" Reg leaned in. "What do you mean?"

"There was a missing piece. I figured the old folks wouldn't mind, so I boxed it up and took it to the care home. Later, I found the last piece in the fridge."

Dan wrinkled his brow. "The fridge?"

"Yeah." She shrugged. "I chalked it up to Mom's dementia. Now, here I am, one of those old folks. Already."

"Well, our puzzle taught *us* a lesson, too, didn't it, Danny?" Reggie grinned.

"Several, I think. About honesty, among other things."

"Anyway, it couldn't have been the same puzzle as yours, honey," Reg added. "Ours was a unique puzzle—that's what Mum called it. And she knew what she was talking about."

"That's right—I remember now." Dan tied up his bag. "Mum told us how puzzles were a big deal during the Depression and owning a one-of-a-kind was a mark of prestige. Chances of yours being the same one are probably . . . one in a million?"

"Yes, I suppose you're right." Setting her cup aside, Felicity unscrewed her thermos. "Probably just similar."

"So did you ever reunite the piece from the fridge with the box at the care home?" Reg removed his gloves and wiped a sleeve across his brow.

"I sure did. I wonder if anyone ever finished it." She reached for the extra travel mugs she'd brought along. "You boys ready for some hot chocolate?"

Chapter Thirty-One

Sunday morning, Dean Jacobs sat at his kitchen table with a cup of coffee, toast, and the *Winnipeg Free Press*. Time for a quick perusal before leaving for church.

The obituary would never have caught his eye if it hadn't included photos of the deceased artist's work. Whoever had submitted this write-up must have spent a bundle. There was no photo of the man himself—Raymond Matthews—but three photos of his artwork graced the page in full color. Dean was no art expert, but the style of the paintings reminded him so much of that crazy old jigsaw puzzle, he read the whole obituary. Turned out, the man was a hundred and four years old and had been a volunteer at the very thrift shop where Dean had taken his stuff—including the puzzle.

Raymond Matthews had studied art for a short time at the University of Manitoba in the 1930s but had to leave school when his father died. The person who wrote the obit obviously held the old guy in high esteem, going on about how he sacrificed for his mother and younger sister. He'd painted pictures for a jigsaw puzzle-maker—*well, that settled it*—and served in World War II. In his later years, Matthews had moved to Winnipeg where he resumed his craft, donating his original paintings to the beloved thrift shop where he volunteered until his passing. Nothing was said about the years in between except that he'd resided in his hometown of Wishing Well. Another uncanny clue. This had to be the same guy.

Ray Matthews lingered on Dean's mind as he sat through church with Samantha and Jack. He pulled a pen from his pocket and tried taking notes on the back of the church bulletin to help him stay focused. The pastor, a young man in casual jeans and a sweater, preached on the verse in the first chapter of Philippians about being confident that when God begins a good work in you, he'll carry it on to completion until the day of Christ Jesus. Dean wasn't sure what "the day of Christ Jesus" meant, but he couldn't help thinking again of that old man's obituary. A hundred and four years was a long time to live. Plenty of time to begin a good work.

But was any amount of time enough to complete what's begun?

"God always finishes what he starts," the preacher said. "You may not see it right now. You may not even see it in your lifetime. You may not see it even when others can. But it's a promise. God put you here to bless others, and he will complete what he began in you."

Dean had reexamined his regrets more times than he could count. If he'd stayed away from alcohol, if he'd stuck it out with Marianne, if he'd quit chasing the corporate dream, if he'd gotten involved in Compassion and Habitat for Humanity sooner— think of the difference he could have made. Now he was trying to play catch-up, but he'd never really catch up. He was already fifty-eight years old.

Then again, if he lived to a hundred and four...or even eighty-four...who knew what God might still do through him? Would the Lord keep using old Ray Matthews' gift to the world now that he'd left it? Dean felt sure of it. Then why was it so hard to believe God could do the same through Dean?

Monday morning before work, Leesha checked eBay, and her mouth fell open. Her puzzle had climbed to more than three hundred dollars in bids. "Oh my goodness!" Her hand flew to her heart. She'd never made that much on anything. Her mother's question about feeling guilty came to mind and immediately had the undesired effect. She had paid fifty cents for the puzzle.

"I'll make a donation to the thrift store," she told her reflection as she swept her black curls up and fastened them with a giant clip. "I promise."

She grabbed her purse and keys from the kitchen table and headed out. "I'm just not promising how *big* of a donation."

On her lunch break, Leesha checked eBay again. The bids were approaching five hundred dollars. Somebody really wanted that puzzle. At least two somebodies, or the number wouldn't keep rising. How could it be worth so much? What did these bidders know that she had missed? Once again, the old man's eerie words came to mind, and Leesha had a hard time concentrating on her work the rest of the afternoon. Between his odd warning, the connection to her mother's ex-husband, and now these wild bids, this puzzle held a mystery begging to be solved. She had to find that old man and discover what he'd meant.

"Heading home already?" a co-worker asked when Leesha gathered up her things at five. "You never leave this early."

"Making an exception today." Leesha smiled and walked quickly to her car. She needed to get to the thrift shop before they closed at five-thirty. Would the old man be there? Had the coffee lady mentioned which days he volunteered?

She barely made it, but the front doors were still open, and the same friendly lady was there, working the till. *Perfect.* Leesha couldn't remember the woman's name, but she marched straight to the cashier's counter and checked her name tag. *Paula. Right.*

Paula finished helping her customer and turned to Leesha. "Well, hello again."

"Hi, Paula. I was shopping here Saturday before last—"

"I remember. You know we don't take returns, right?"

"Oh! Yes, I know that."

"What can I do for you?"

"Well, I was wondering..." If only she could remember the old man's name. "The gentleman who spoke to me that day, the one you said was a hundred and four—would he, by any chance, be here now? I really need to ask him something."

The woman stared at her a moment. "I'm afraid he's not here today." Was it Leesha's imagination, or had the woman's face suddenly turned pale?

"I wasn't sure which days he's here, so I thought I'd take a chance. Do you know when he'll be here?"

"I'm afraid Ray won't be back with us, love."

Now it was Leesha's turn to stare. *Ray. That was it.* "Is he ... sick?"

"Actually ... Ray passed away on Friday night," Paula said gently. "We're closing the store on Wednesday for his funeral."

Leesha felt her shoulders sag. "I'm so sorry."

"Was there something I can help you with?"

"Um. No. No, thank you." Leesha turned to leave. "I'm very sorry for your loss."

On her way out, a bright orange sign on the door caught her eye.

Corner Thrift will be closed Wednesday afternoon, April 26,
for the funeral of our long-time volunteer, Ray Matthews.
Anyone who knew and loved Ray is welcome to attend.

Leesha hadn't known or loved the man, but how weird would it be to attend out of curiosity? She shook off the thought. She couldn't very well ask to be excused from work to attend a stranger's funeral.

But she did make note of the time and place.

Dan Gordon hadn't talked to Reggie and Felicity since Saturday, but he couldn't shake the memories they had discussed at the cemetery. Reminiscing about the jigsaw puzzle and Mum's radio reminded him what a wonderful woman she'd been. He hadn't realized until he became a parent himself how much responsibility she'd had on her shoulders. Most of the younger war widows he knew had remarried, but Mum had soldiered on alone. She'd supported Dan through university and Reggie through Bible school. She'd been a good grandmother to his girls when they were little, but she grew ill and died much too young for Dan's daughters to have many memories of her.

Next week would mark forty years since pancreatic cancer took her. Maybe he'd do one of those memorial ads in the newspaper, just to honor her. It was a small gesture that few would read, but the idea wouldn't let him go. He grabbed Monday's paper to find one he could use as an example. If he submitted his tomorrow, it could run on the anniversary of her death, April 30.

He opened the newspaper to the *Passages* page. He'd always told himself he'd never become one of those old geezers who deliberately checked the obituaries every morning to see if any acquaintances had passed—at least, not until he reached eighty or eighty-five. But he had to admit, it was becoming harder to resist. In recent years, more and more retired teachers passed— his former colleagues. He scanned them now, telling himself he really wasn't reading them.

Someone had submitted an obituary with no photo of the deceased. Odd. Instead, three pictures of artwork graced the ad. Dan stared at them. He'd seen this style before, but where? He closed his eyes, and the old puzzle of the girl at the wishing well sprung to mind—surely, because they'd just been discussing it. It had been on his mind, and now his mind was playing tricks. Still, he read the obit. The artist's name was Ray Matthews, and he'd been born in nineteen-thirteen.

… during the Depression years, Ray supported his mother and sister by selling his artwork to a jigsaw puzzle-maker.

Dan read it twice more. Oh, if only Mum was still around. She'd worked for one of those companies. How many could there have been? The obituary went on to state that the man had continued volunteering at a local thrift store until his passing, and that the store was accepting donations to a trust fund Matthews had initiated.

In lieu of flowers, donations may be made to the Ray Matthews Memorial Scholarship Fund, which will be used to send deserving young artists to art school.

The remainder of the obituary gave details for a funeral service to be held Wednesday at four o'clock. Dan checked his watch. If he hurried, he could still make it.

Chapter Thirty-Two

*D*an arrived just in time to slip into a back pew before the advertised start time. *You're losing it, old man. Going to a funeral for someone you've never met. You really need to get a life.*

A slide show played at the front of the stage, photos of complete strangers scrolling, one after the other, some of them dating back to the nineteen-twenties. It didn't take long to figure out which one was Ray Matthews. There were few early photos from his childhood and youth. Just one with a young lady. Although the image was too old for Dan to make out their faces clearly, something looked familiar about the girl. They posed like sweethearts, though the obit had stated that Ray had never married. One shot of Ray in uniform, hand on an army jeep, reminded Dan of the father he knew only from photos.

Then the pictures seemed to take a leap into the fifties when Ray would have been middle-aged. Sixties, seventies, eighties styles faded in and out to instrumental hymns as the photos improved in quality. Suddenly, one picture jumped out at Dan, causing his breath to catch in his throat. Ray, already elderly, stood next to a high school graduate. Dan would recognize the smiling co-ed anywhere. She was the young lady from the old wishing well puzzle! It made no sense. If Ray did paint that puzzle, he'd have done it decades before that girl was born. How was that possible?

Then he looked down the row and across the aisle. There sat his own sister-in-law, Felicity! Had he walked into some kind of Twilight Zone? He wanted to change seats and find out what she was doing there, but just as he stood, the whole congregation rose with him. The family members of the deceased were filing in. Dan folded his hands in front of him and waited respectfully. An assortment of couples who looked to be in their seventies and eighties led the procession, followed by the next generation of middle-agers, then a handful of young parents with little kids. Impressive. For someone who never married, Ray Matthews had a large family. His obit had listed as survivors only nephews and nieces.

The family took their seats, and the congregation was invited to do the same. Dan mumbled along with the hymns that followed, still thinking about the woman from the puzzle. *You are definitely losing your mind, Danny Gordon.*

Felicity sang along to "Amazing Grace," remembering Mama's funeral so many years ago. She'd never met Ray Matthews, but she'd run into a former student at the grocery store and promised him she'd attend the first funeral he conducted as a care pastor at his church. Luke appeared so at ease as he took the pulpit, Felicity doubted he really needed her support.

"Good afternoon, everyone. My name is Luke Broadfoot, and I'm a pastor here. On behalf of Ray Matthews' family, I want to thank you all for coming today to celebrate his life. It's no secret that his was a long one. On his one hundredth birthday just over four years ago, we held a party for him right here in this church. I asked Ray what the secret to his long life was. His response was priceless—'just keep getting up every morning.'"

The congregation chuckled.

"On Saturday morning, Ray Matthews got up to find himself in glory. I believe he'd want us to celebrate that, although we'll miss him down here. I'd like to call on his niece, Pearl Martindale, to deliver the eulogy."

A smartly dressed woman walked to the platform and stood behind the pulpit. "I'm the youngest of Uncle Ray's nieces and nephews," she began. "And even *I'm* getting up there!"

The crowd responded with soft laughter again. Felicity noticed very few heads without gray or white hair, except those that had no hair at all.

"The portrait you see here of Uncle Ray was done by my daughter, Naomi Martindale. She couldn't be with us today because she has an exhibit opening in Halifax where she lives. But she was so pleased to know her painting was chosen to display in this place of honor." Pearl motioned to the closed casket in front of her, on which rested a bouquet of spring flowers and a beautifully framed portrait of a smiling old man with a twinkle in his eye. "Ray was still a youngster of ninety when Naomi painted this for an art class in university. I asked her why she chose Uncle Ray, of all subjects. 'I've never seen a face with so much character,' was her answer. And I suppose that about sums up the truth of who Ray Matthews was—a real character."

This time, Felicity joined the crowd in an appreciative chuckle.

"My mother, Caroline, was Ray's only sibling," Pearl continued. "She once told me he'd been her hero as a young girl. He dropped out of art school during the Depression, when their father died, to keep the farm going. He painted pictures for extra income. She said he literally saved her life as a sickly young girl. He fought for our country in World War II. And in his hometown of Wishing Well, he was known as the builder and keeper of the official wishing well in the town square, created in memory of my husband's aunt, Sarah Martindale. Legend has it that Uncle Ray was engaged to Sarah when she passed away at nineteen years of age.

"At some point, Uncle Ray and my mother had a bit of a falling out, and we didn't see much of him. Oh, he'd come around for family gatherings, bringing us kids gifts. Mom described him as a temperamental artist, 'all temper and half mental.' I never knew what their disagreement was about, but somewhere along the way—around the time I married—Uncle Ray and Mom tore down their fences. I'm so glad they did. Ray became dearer to us than ever, and I'm so thankful we've had the privilege of having him in our lives these past forty years and in our neighborhood for nearly twenty. I asked him once if he regretted anything about his long life. His response was that he waited too long to reconcile with his sister and to embrace the joy of knowing the Lord.

"Then he said something that has really stuck with me, and I hope you'll remember it too. He said he'd learned that Jesus Christ is the last piece to every puzzle. I thought that was interesting, coming from a guy whose artwork was used to create jigsaw puzzles. 'What do you mean, Uncle Ray?' I asked him.

"'Doesn't matter what your problem is,' he said. 'Doesn't matter what pieces seem to be missing from your life. It doesn't even matter what religion you are. Jesus is, and always will be, the last piece that completes everything.' I wish I'd figured that out sooner, but I'm glad Jesus brought me to the truth of it.'

"On behalf of the family, I want to thank this congregation for making Uncle Ray an important part of our church family, and Pastor Luke for handling all the arrangements with such compassion and professionalism. A huge thank you to his special friend, Mabel Peterson, and to all the staff and volunteers at Corner Thrift. Ray saw you all as family too. I really believe you helped give his life purpose and meaning, and you're one of the big reasons he lived to a hundred and four. Thanks so much for coming."

The woman took her seat, and Felicity focused again on her former student as he took the pulpit. Luke gave a brief message from Second Timothy Four, where Paul said, "I have fought the good fight, I have finished the race, I have kept the faith. Now there is in store for me the crown of righteousness, which the Lord, the righteous Judge, will award to me on that day—and not only to me, but also to all who have longed for his appearing."

Luke made eye contact with Felicity once during his talk, and his smile made her glad she'd come. He'd been part of her very last graduating class in ninety-nine, so he'd be around thirty-six years old now. Her heart swelled with pride for him.

When the family headed out, Felicity turned her attention to the slide show replaying at the front. She immediately did a double-take when the photo of a young graduate came up. Where had she seen that face before? How could she possibly know that girl—was it one of her students? No. Felicity had an instant image of a young woman with daisies in her hair, gazing down a wishing well. The picture changed, and Felicity shook the thought away.

That's when she spotted her brother-in-law Danny across the aisle. *What on earth?*

They met in the middle.

"What brings you here?" Dan asked as they walked out together.

"I could ask you the same thing." Felicity pulled on her mittens. "The pastor is one of my former students. I ran into him yesterday. We got to chatting, and he confided how nervous he was about doing his first funeral today. I said I'd come support him. I know, it's weird."

Dan shook his head. "Not as weird as what brought me."

They stood off to the side at the back of the sanctuary while Dan explained how Ray Matthews' obituary had caught his eye because of his paintings, and how he'd become convinced Ray was the same artist who created the jigsaw puzzle they'd been discussing just days before.

"I know it's crazy." He looked down at the funeral program in his hands. "Then I'm watching the slide show, and I swear, I see the same girl from the puzzle on the screen. I'm losing it, Felicity. Maybe it's time you and Reggie had me committed somewhere."

Felicity put her hand on his arm. "I saw it, too, Dan. The girl from my mother's puzzle! Are we both nuts?"

They watched the slide show loop around until the picture came again.

"That's her!" They said it in unison.

"It makes no sense, though." Dan wrinkled his brow. "The puzzle's too old, and the photo's too recent."

Felicity sighed. "Family resemblance? Maybe the girl in the graduation gown is a descendent of the girl at the wishing well?"

"Mmm...maybe."

They walked through the foyer together and waited on the sidewalk as Ray's casket was loaded into a hearse.

"I guess we'll never know for sure." Dan held his hand over his heart in respect.

Felicity just nodded.

Chapter Thirty-Three

For the second time that week, Leesha Pennington left the office before five. She headed straight to the church where the funeral service would be underway for Ray Matthews. Sometimes, funerals were long, drawn-out affairs. Could she make it in time to learn anything about the strange old man? Find any clues as to what his odd warning might have meant? Or would she simply find out he'd suffered from dementia and rarely made sense?

But as she approached the church, the hearse pulled away from the curb. A cortege of half a dozen cars followed, and Leesha pulled over to wait. Then, as if propelled by some force beyond her will, she turned her steering wheel and joined the procession.

"You're crazy, Leesha," she muttered. "You should go home. Get some work done."

But she kept following. The hearse pulled onto a main thoroughfare and sped up. The cars followed, and so did Leesha. "This is ridiculous." She glanced in the rearview mirror. "What if they're headed to some cemetery out in the country, an hour away?" She made up her mind she'd follow for another ten minutes and if they hadn't turned off, she'd take the nearest exit and go home.

But blinkers soon started flashing for a right turn, and Leesha followed the other cars down a service road to Creekside Cemetery. "What will I do when everyone else gets out of their vehicles?" She checked her reflection. "You can be so silly, you know that?"

She slowed down, and when the procession began to pull over, she hung back so she could park farther away. She watched while the casket was unloaded and carried by six men to a freshly dug grave, followed by maybe twenty-five people. They gathered around, and a minister opened what she presumed to be a Bible. She rolled her window down, but his voice was so faint, she couldn't make out what he was saying.

Fifteen minutes later, the casket had been lowered, and the people returned to their vehicles. One by one, they pulled away. This time, Leesha didn't follow. She continued to watch until even the pastor left. Then two cemetery workers came along, one with a shovel and one with a mini excavator, to fill in the grave. Leesha pulled her phone out of her purse and checked her eBay account. With three hours left for bids, the puzzle price rose toward eight hundred dollars.

"This can't be right. This just can't be right." She kept muttering as she logged out and back in. This had to be a glitch. The money would make a nice, big dent in her debt, but she did not feel good about it. "You're cheating the thrift store. Or somebody." With a sigh, she returned the phone to her purse. The workers had finished their task and were leaving the gravesite. The clock on her dashboard read five-fifty-five.

"Okay, Ray Matthews." She put her hand on the door handle. "You and I need to chat."

She waited until the workers were out of sight before climbing out of her Buick and walking over to the grave. Only a small, temporary sign from the funeral home identified the man whose body lay below. Leesha stared at it for several minutes, glanced about to make sure no one was around, and began to speak.

"Mr. Matthews? You don't know me, but my name is Leesha Pennington. I bought an old puzzle from your thrift store last week. They sure like you there, by the way. I don't know why we never met before. I'm in there most Saturdays, but maybe that's not your regular day. Anyway. You said something bizarre about the puzzle, and now it's got me rattled. What did you know about it?"

Leesha stopped talking, honestly hoping she'd receive some sort of revelation. Nothing came. Birds twittered in the nearby trees. Although the April days were lengthening, the sun was low in the west against a blue backdrop.

"I want you to know two things," Leesha continued. "For one, we finished the puzzle. My parents and I, Friday evening. Same day you died. It was beautiful. My mother took a picture, wants to make a quilt. Knowing her, she'll do it too. It seems like that crazy puzzle helped bring my parents to a new and better place in their marriage. So … I just wanted you to know.

"And the second thing is …" Her eyes scanned the treetops. "There are at least two eBay bidders who want the puzzle pretty bad. I don't know why. But I don't feel right about keeping the money. I want you to know I'm giving it back to the thrift shop. Maybe they'll put it toward that scholarship fund they're handling in your memory, to help starving artists or whatever. I don't know, but I'm sure it'll go to a worthy cause. So … yeah. That's what I'm going to do. I promise."

Leesha stood a moment longer before walking back to her car for the drive home. She'd probably never know what the old man had meant, but she'd come to a conclusion. She was not going to tell her mother she had cyber-stalked Dean Jacobs.

Dean left the newspaper office where he'd dropped off the memorial notice in honor of Mum. Ray Matthews' obituary and mysterious puzzle had refused to leave his mind. He'd even stopped at Corner Thrift that morning to see if the puzzle was still there, but it had been sold. Now he found himself headed toward the church mentioned in the obituary. The funeral would surely be over, but maybe he'd find one of those printed programs left behind in the church lobby—something that could shed a little light on the artist's life.

Not only were the front doors hanging open, but people were still milling around. In the lobby, Dean took a program and looked at the photos on display and the paintings resting on easels. The style was the same. Dean was no art expert, but he just knew Ray Matthews was the creator of that girl at the wishing well. He had to be.

Dean drew the line at signing the guest book and turned to leave.

"Attention, everyone." A young man wearing a clerical collar spoke from the top of a stairwell. "The family has returned from the interment, and you're all invited to join us downstairs for some refreshments and more reminiscing about Ray." He looked directly at Dean.

The jig's up. He knows I'm a fraud.

The man smiled. "Please join us."

With no idea what compelled him, Dean followed several others to the basement where the smells of coffee and sandwiches greeted him. He found a space along one wall to lean. A smiling woman came around with a tray holding disposable cups full of red punch. Dean took one, just for something to hold. The pastor welcomed everyone and said the microphone was open for anyone who wanted to share their favorite memories about Ray.

A woman who looked vaguely familiar wasted no time walking to the mic.

"My name is Paula, and I volunteer at Corner Thrift." One hand fluttered around her amble bosom.

Ah, yes. That's where he'd seen her. The day he dropped the puzzle off.

"I believe it was my mother Mabel who first convinced Ray to help out at the shop ages ago," the woman said. "Some of you know Mom and Ray struck up a special friendship and we're thankful for the companionship they shared. It wasn't until I retired and started volunteering myself that I really got to know Ray. By then, he'd become a permanent fixture. He was the one you went to when you had a question or couldn't find something. He just always seemed to know. We sure will miss him.

"In the last couple of years, Ray began saying the oddest things. We never knew if he was sharing snippets of wisdom or deep, dark secrets from his past or what. Sometimes, we just wrote it off as old age, but other times, I really wondered.

"I asked him one day—because I knew he'd been a bachelor all his life, you see—I asked him, 'Ray, were you ever in love?'

"You know what he said? One word. He goes, 'Forever.' Just like that. 'Forever.'

"Now, I ask you—what does that mean? I couldn't tell you. Then he'd change the subject. He was always bragging about his grand-niece, Naomi Martindale. 'Famous artist,' he said. I never heard of her. 'She got my artistic ability and her aunt Sarah's beauty,' he'd say. Which made no sense because Ray never married.

"But I do know this. Ray Matthews loved the Lord. He wanted to serve him any way he could. And those paintings of his? Well, my, oh my, don't you know those beautiful paintings are blessing people in homes all over this city? Maybe all over the country!"

The woman opened her mouth to go on, but the pastor gently leaned into the microphone. "Thanks, Paula. Would anyone else like to share? Let's try to keep it to a minute or so, shall we, so everyone who wants to share can get a chance?"

Dean slowly made his way out of the room and up the stairs while another thrift shop volunteer talked about Ray. When he reached his car, Dean sat a moment before heading home. He didn't need to know all the details about that puzzle. It was enough that it had once taught him a lesson in letting go.

Leesha dumped canned soup on the stove to heat while she changed out of her suit and into her beloved yoga pants. It was seven by the time she finished eating and tidying her little kitchen. With one last good stare at the beautiful girl at the wishing well, she carefully bubble-wrapped it and placed it inside another box for shipping. She taped it securely with packing tape, then stuck on an address label and got out her black, fine-tip marker. She could have it on its way tomorrow, and she'd deliver a check to Corner Thrift as soon as the money showed up in her account.

She opened her laptop, her heart beating wildly as she watched the closing moments of her eBay auction. The price had risen some more, and finally ended at eight o'clock. The buyer was prepared to pay nine hundred and thirty dollars!

Her email dinged and she clicked on it. *Great news. Your item sold. Now it's time to get it ready.*

Ping! Ping! A second email from eBay told her the buyer had paid. Another from Paypal said the money was in her account.

She opened her eBay account and clicked on *View Order Details* to discover the identity of the person who had purchased the puzzle for such an exorbitant sum.

Thursday morning, Leesha stopped at Corner Thrift with a donation of nine hundred dollars, even. They were thrilled to receive it and agreed to put it toward the Raymond Matthews Memorial Art Scholarship fund. Her next stop was the post office, where the remaining thirty dollars bought enough postage to cover the shipping of the antique puzzle.

She double-checked the label she had carefully addressed to the winning bidder—Naomi Martindale of Halifax, Nova Scotia. She placed the label on the package and slid it across the counter and on its way with a silent prayer. *Lord, may this puzzle bless Naomi Martindale—whoever she is—in a way that's worth every penny and more. Amen.*

Note to the Reader

Ironically, I've never been a fan of jigsaw puzzles. In a wild moment of reckless abandon in 2017, I opened a thousand-piece puzzle on our dining table. I thought my husband and I could complete it over the Christmas break and share a little bonding time in the process. A year later, the unfinished puzzle still sat on that table. We'd covered it with a tablecloth on several occasions when we needed the space. Finally, in defeat, I returned the pieces to their box.

That incident, along with a fascination for seemingly random stories that all converge in the end, provided my inspiration for *The Last Piece*. I hope you enjoyed it enough to look at the Discussion Questions at the end, and to leave a review on Amazon, Goodreads, or wherever you can.

For further reading, check out my author page on Amazon, where you'll find my other books. I'd love to hear from you on Facebook or via email at terriejtodd@gmail.com. You can also subscribe to my Author Newsletter on my blog site at www.terrietodd.blogspot.com or simply email me and I'll add you. Thanks for reading!

God bless you,
Terrie Todd

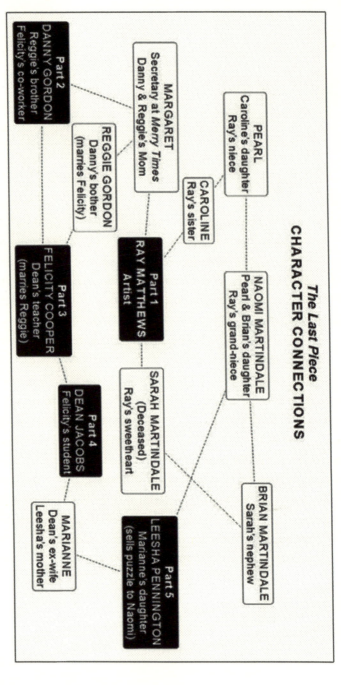

The Last Piece
CHARACTER CONNECTIONS

Part 2
DANNY GORDON
Reggie's brother
Felicity's co-worker

MARGARET
Secretary at *Merry Times*
Danny & Reggie's Mom

PEARL
Caroline's daughter
Ray's niece

REGGIE GORDON
Danny's brother
(marries Felicity)

CAROLINE
Ray's sister

Part 1
RAY MATTHEWS
Artist

NAOMI MARTINDALE
Pearl & Brian's daughter
Ray's grand-niece

Part 3
FELICITY COOPER
Dean's teacher
(marries Reggie)

SARAH MARTINDALE
(Deceased)
Ray's sweetheart

Part 4
DEAN JACOBS
Felicity's student

BRIAN MARTINDALE
Sarah's nephew

MARIANNE
Dean's ex-wife
Leesha's mother

Part 5
LEESHA PENNINGTON
Marianne's daughter
(sells puzzle to Naomi)

Acknowledgements

They say writing is a solitary effort, but every book is a group project and I have lots of people to thank. Kathy Letkeman, your expert nursing advice and consistent encouragement mean more than you know. Kevin Hamm, you run the best thrift shop anywhere! Thanks for helping me give Ray a role in my fictional one. Carol Dyck Foster, you provided even more than I needed to know about selling goods online. Thanks for sharing your secrets!

Denise Weimer, my editor, it's a joy to work with you. Clarise Klassen, your eagle eye is appreciated almost as much as your friendship. Gayle Loewen, your ability to shoot an attractive headshot boosts my self-confidence. Thank you, Ginny Smith and the team at Books & Such Literary Agency for all your assistance on this project. And Mary DeMuth, agent, advisor, mentor, encourager, and friend, thanks for keeping me going! Love and thanks to Jon who gets to hear my wailing and gnashing of teeth when I want to quit.

Above all, my thanks are due to my redeemer, Jesus Christ, master storyteller and main character in the greatest story ever told.

Book Club Discussion Guide

1. Even though he was such a young man, Ray stubbornly clung to the memory of his deceased sweetheart to the point of obsession. Why do you think he found it so difficult to move on? Do you know anyone who has lived their life this way? What would you say to them?

2. When Ray finally agreed to sell his painting of Sarah, he pronounced a type of spell over it. Do you believe his prophecy came true? Do you believe humans hold this kind of power?

3. Most young war widows remarried, but Danny and Reggie Gordon's mother remained a single mother. Do you think this was a choice on her part? Why or why not?

4. Felicity Cooper shared a close bond with her mother. Do you think it was healthy? Why or why not?

5. Dean Jacob's life seemed defined by bitterness and failure. He lost both parents, his infant daughter, his marriage, and his sobriety. When we encounter him again, we discover the rich and meaningful ways his life blessed others. What do you think contributed to the turn-around?

6. Consider the character Leesha Pennington. How would you describe her?

7. In many ways, the puzzle becomes a main character in this book. Is it the villain? The hero? A little of both?

8. All five stories converge near the end of the book. Was it hard to keep the characters straight? Did you find the ending satisfying?

9. If you could give a word of advice to just one character in this book, who would you choose and what would you say?

10. Ray told Pearl that, "Jesus is, and always will be, the last piece that completes everything." If that's true, what might that mean for your life?

Made in the USA
Middletown, DE
23 November 2021

52883797R00151